THE DESERT TALON

KARIN LOWACHEE

SOLARIS

First published 2025 by Solaris
an imprint of Rebellion Publishing Ltd,
Riverside House, Osney Mead,
Oxford, OX2 0ES, UK

www.solarisbooks.com

ISBN: 978-1-83786-402-7

10 9 8 7 6 5 4 3 2 1

A CIP catalogue record for this book is available from the
British Library.

Designed & typeset by Rebellion Publishing

Printed in Denmark

To the readers following along from Book One
Thank you
And to all the new readers
Thank you

THE GUARD CAME for him in the early hours. Watery blue dawn washed through the bars in the window like a slow tide and brought the cold and the muted sound of distant suon calling to the morning. Even through the sense-dampening caul cast over the prison, Janan recognized Tourmaline's staccato trill, as every morning for the past three months his suon had threatened the world for his freedom. The Mazoön officials had told him they were keeping Tourmaline in an aviary nearby, that she could see the sky like he could see it through the iron bars of his cell, as if the tease of liberty could truly comfort. This place was supposed to be a temporary holding but at least a hundred dawns had come and gone, and in this one came the guard. Janan recognized him as a Mazoön man named Sooly, who had been neither cruel nor kind, but looked on Janan as one would a camp dog.

He roused himself from the narrow cot on which he tried to sleep every night, but the ever-present pressure in his mind from the prison's caul had created a grout of discomfort he could not smooth out. It left his thoughts in a thick muddle, and as he moved, his limbs groused at the energy required. Some hours he felt like this place was whittling him to the quick. Anger swirled in eddies with the abiding frustration, but it had no channel for overflow. Once in a while Sooly told him that his case was being reviewed, but he had no confirmation if that was true.

Sooly's incandescent white keys hummed like hammer-struck metal as he walked behind Janan. Their footsteps on the smooth, scarred floor became a syncopated accompaniment to the low steady note of Mazoön potency even contained in such small objects. They passed a prisoner in faded denim coveralls sweeping dust from the corners. The sound of the broom pushing and tapping joined them in the symphonic score of their passage. She looked up once with dark hollowed eyes and Janan met her stare. She looked back down and continued in her endless tidying like some lower deity punished for stepping above her station. Every sound echoed through the narrow stone corridors with their windowless doors and locked iron gates in regular intervals, checkpoints along a path to the nether end of death. Each time a gate opened and shut the buzz of Mazoön mythicism threw small shockwaves toward him and peppered his back as he passed through.

His tongue felt ashen in his mouth. Sooly hadn't given him a moment before this excursion to drink water from the sink in his cell. "Where are we going?"

The Mazoön didn't answer. They passed through another gate and came abruptly to a door. Sooly guided him inside a room arranged as if for diners in some macabre celebration. In the center, a black rough-hewn table and four black chairs, two each on the long edges, as if the trees from which they'd been constructed had grown from volcanic basalt and remained of that nature. A woman and a creature made of metal and polished wood sat in the two chairs facing the door. Janan paused. Sooly gave his back a small push toward the table and the woman gestured to the rightmost empty seat across from herself.

He heard the door shut behind him and the shockwave undulated up his back like phantom fingers. Locked. Sooly left him alone in here with the woman and the metal creature who sat, eyeless, in the shape of a man, its jaw hinged with brass. A skull face and a skeleton's body of polished pewter and glazed dark wood. A barebones man flayed of skin.

"Please sit," the woman said in a halting attempt at his Ba'Suon dialect. "Sephihalé. Sit."

"What is that?"

She didn't look at the creature. "My recordkeeper. It won't harm you. Please sit so we can begin."

He had seen very little of Mazoön mythicism, as they called it, once he'd entered their country beyond the silos and checkpoints around the island that tracked and barred all incursions from across the long waters. It was why he was in this prison, as the moment he'd crossed their borders an alarm of some kind had alerted them in their posts of defense. Had he known the extent of their surveillance and paranoia he would have kept going in his flight from Kattaka. All he'd heard through the war was that the Mazoön accepted Ba'Suon knowing, though they looked on it as inferior, and they didn't desire to use it or control it like the Kattakans did. Still, he'd fought Mazemoor in the war and didn't think they'd be amenable to his presence, but Tourmaline had brought him here as if she somehow remembered this land. Perhaps she did through her ancestors.

The Greatmothers of the families told stories of long ago when the Mazoön and Ba'Suon were one people. Such stories had the temper of fiction but he knew now they were true: he caught glimpses of similarities in the countenance of the people he met here, even Sooly. A certain energetic whisper in their presence, like passing through a room where recently there'd been a congregation. Not even the suppression of the caul around this prison could extinguish it from his knowing. But any such past commonality hadn't sped his incarceration in this land.

"Sephihalé," said the woman again. "Or do you prefer drere Janan?"

"Drere is a Mazoön word." Their interpretation of the Kattakan *dragoneer*, a word he did not claim. But she knew his family name and spoke his language in a serviceable manner. He yanked back the chair and sat.

She was older than him, he guessed, though Mazoön

in their city living seemed to age in acceleration. Deep lines beneath her eyes as if all the world she'd witnessed now weighed on her face. Long dark hair coiled to a crown on top of her head and strung through with fine copper wire. The red-painted slash of a mouth, the color extending from ear to ear, bisecting her cheeks. Her tar-black eyes evaluated him as though his very existence was some sort of test to her.

"I didn't know Ba'Suon could be blond," she said in a tone of vague curiosity.

"Do you have a smoke?" he said.

Her finely drawn eyebrows arched in surprise. Maybe to her, Ba'Suon didn't smoke either. She reached into the breast pocket of her gray, form-fitting jacket and produced a thin silver case of cigarettes. She held it out to him and he extracted a stick and lightly pinched it between his fingers as she withdrew a small box of matches of the kind he'd seen in Kattaka. She struck a match on the box and lit the cigarette for him. He pulled on it and settled back, crossing an arm over his stomach. The smoke was surprisingly smooth.

She watched him for a moment then cleared her throat and looked at the pewter man. "Recordkeeper, begin archive." It made a strange grinding noise and the brass jaw dropped open. As the woman began to speak, a slow roll of yellow paper began to spit from its mouth like a snake tongue. The angular scratch of the Mazoön written language manifested on the sheet as though burned there by fine points of fire. The cavern from which the pewter man expelled the paper glowed a dull gold. Janan set his hand on the edge of the black table and leaned away as far as he could, missing the first few phrases of the woman's speech. "...you of the terms and conditions upon your release," she said.

That drew his attention from her alarming companion. "My release?"

"Yes, drere Janan. I've been assigned your case and we are in the process of negotiating your release from provisional holding."

"You mean this prison."

"You aren't a prisoner. You're a refugee from Kattaka and have been treated as such. Kattaka, may I remind you, who instigated a war with Mazemoor for a decade."

"I'm aware."

"A war in which you fought on their side. We have reason to be cautious."

"It was that or an internment camp. Then they threatened me with execution when I wanted to leave the army. I told your officers when I first came here with my suon."

"I'm aware." She smiled. It made the red bar of her mouth paint tilt askew. "According to your initial statement, you waited five years before you fled their country. Why is that, if they had threatened you post-war?"

"I was waiting out the contract of someone in my unit. We were going to leave together."

"You didn't want to go home to your people at the conclusion of the war?"

He stared at her. In that brief silence, the pewter man fell silent. The room hummed and his headache pressed in. "My people are all scattered."

"So when did the situation become dire?"

"When they said they would take my suon and if I didn't co-operate they would execute me. I just told you—"

"Yes, but the fact of the matter is, drere Janan, you fought against Mazemoor in a war that killed many of our people. You possess a powerful form of mythicism and a battle-trained suon. You can't expect us to just let you loose on our country merely on your say-so. While you've been in holding, the Department of State has reviewed your case and monitored your behavior."

He remembered the burning cigarette and smoked it. The pewter man spat its roll of yellow paper, chronicling all of their words. "How'd I do?"

"Very well. Which is why I'm here to inform you of the terms of your release. May I continue?"

She asked as if she hadn't been the one interrogating him just now. He tilted his chin up.

She turned a page in the file of papers on the table in front of her. He couldn't read the Mazoön words but he saw his photograph pasted on one of the sheets. They had taken his image from him when he'd first arrived, made him stand for interminable minutes in front of a painted canvas sheet of some indistinct forestry. The first of many bizarre contrivances in this country.

"As you say," she continued, "your participation

in the war was under a certain amount of duress. We are also aware that it was Kattaka that sought to invade us, not the Ba'Suon families. We have taken this into account. We have also taken into account the testimonies of other Ba'Suon who have sought asylum in Mazemoor to be free from the Kattakan regime in your homeland. One such Ba'Suon is a member of your family tribe. Her name is Sephihalé ele Prita."

He set both hands on the black table. The smoke from his cigarette carved upwards, making calligraphy in the air. "Prita's in Mazemoor?"

"Yes. It says here she filed for asylum a couple of years into the war. She deserted her Kattakan post. You had no contact with your family once you'd enlisted?"

"Not consistently."

"She's volunteered to sponsor your release. You'll be on probation for a year. A caseworker from the Bureau of Internal Security will be assigned to you in the field with whom you will meet on occasion for assessment and reporting purposes. Your movements will be restricted, as well as your mythicism."

"You keep using that word. It doesn't apply to me."

She drew a breath and laced her hands on top of her stack of papers. "Drere Janan, your people may call it what you will in your own language, but here in Mazemoor we understand it as mythicism. You are an enastramyth, whether you use that word or not."

First the Kattakans categorized the Ba'Suon in order to justify their control. Now these Mazoön. "I don't practice your mythicism. We don't share a common language, and as I understand it, your mythicism traps the world with your words."

"We aren't trying to erase your identity. This is merely for the sake of understanding, and for the record." She glanced at the pewter man.

He pointed to her papers. "Do you call me this 'enastramyth' in your file?"

"A Ba'Suon enastramyth, yes."

"Then it's a lie."

She stared at him as if caught in a thought. He smoked. The pewter man stopped its spitting of paper and looked with its sightless eyeholes toward the blank wall.

She took a deep breath and began again, slowly, as if he might have trouble hearing her words. The pewter man's mouth lit gold. "During this period of probation, any infraction may result in your deportation back to Kattaka. Sephihalé ele Prita would also be held accountable and punishable by law as a landed immigrant of Mazemoor. Do you understand?"

He rolled smoke over his tongue. "I understand." He understood that he was no more free here than he'd been in Kattaka as one of their soldiers.

The woman slid over one of the sheets of paper. "Do you know how to write your name?"

"Yes."

She held out a thin silver stick. He looked at it. "It's a pen," she said. "Put the pointed end to that line there and make your mark."

"I want to know what it says on the paper."

"I just told you."

"There seems to be more words here than what you've told me."

Her mouth went askew again. "I summarized."

"I want to see Prita."

"Sign the paper and you may."

"I want to see my sister in the family." He pushed back the chair and stood, crushing the cigarette on the black table. Ash to ash.

"It would mean you remain in holding for an indefinite amount of time until she can arrive, drere Janan."

He went to the door and banged on it with his fist. The stinging buzz of its lock reverberated up his arm. "I've been here for months already. If you're acting as my advocate you'll bring her here immediately." He looked at the pewter man, eyeless and agape. "It's on record now. How is my suon?"

"I don't know. I would assume it's well."

"Please check on her. I was told she's being held in an aviary on one of the small islands off-shore. She would be registered under the name Tourmaline."

The woman's painted mouth showed only a thin red line now. "Anything else?"

"I would like a pack of cigarettes. A Kattakan brand called Fortune's Fire. As you're in treaty it should not be impossible to acquire." The door unlocked with the deep sound of something exploding beneath leagues of water. He felt the push of it at his shoulder like the nudge of a great whale. On the other side Sooly held his white keys. The weight of the prison's dampening caul crackled against Janan's skin.

They feared what he might do, what his Ba'Suon knowing meant in the paradigm of their mythicism. These Mazoön didn't realize that they could never accurately name something they would never understand.

He dreamed often of his escape from Kattaka, as if in some way his mind and memory both colluded to repaint what had occurred. In his dream Lilley escaped with him and they both flew to their freedom, somewhere south past even Mazemoor, where the sands along the shore shone white both day and night.

But awake and lying on the cot, which only accommodated his height if he bent his knees, he thought of what he'd left behind and how he had left it. Every hour away from the man, whose red hair and stone blue eyes struck him at first glance like some sort of elemental spirit, now possessed the parts of him that had discovered a borderless love. They barely spoke each other's languages in the beginning, but beyond such inadequate fathoms of expression they'd managed an understanding. Through war and the bloodletting of the world, they loved. Beneath the arc of his suon's wings and in the pale gold of a summer's dawn.

His shoulder, where his family's kusha had inked the

mark of their oaths to each other, now ached inside the pressure of the Mazoön caul. In this cell and beneath the roof of this prison he couldn't feel Lilley even in the most delicate strand of knowing, which before had never broken, not even in wild distress and the clamor of battle. But thousands of miles and a world removed from each other and he could not even discern if the other man was alive or dead. He wanted to think that he would know if Lilley were dead, but in this country that pushed his awareness inside itself until most of what he felt was nothing but a hard knot of resistance, he couldn't be sure. He might never know.

The Mazoön had even taken his harwa, the suon bone wristcuff which had passed through generations of his parental line so he could gift it to his beloved. The harwa had been taken from him once before, and he'd barely withstood the shame of the loss. Now the Mazoön kept it 'in storage' until his eventual release, they'd said, but he couldn't feel its existence any more than he felt Lilley's, who should have been the one to wear it. Everything had seemed to slip through his fingers in regular stages of loss since he was nineteen years under the stars and joined the war for his freedom. A freedom that had been a lie.

A night bird called from outside the barred window, on the water surrounding this prison—a low wail, some smaller echo to the sound of his suon. He imagined telling it his thoughts and sending it north to Kattaka where it could perch on Lilley's arm and relay the message. Lilley had always been fond of flying creatures, whether birds or suon, and it had been Tourmaline's affinity for him that had turned Janan's initial skepticism into reluctant acceptance.

He looked up now at the low ceiling cast in shadow, the thick presence of the caul behind his eyes. His fingers stroked a circle around his left wrist, where he should have been wearing his harwa. If he closed his eyes and concentrated, he could almost feel the inlaid pearl and suon bone against his fingertips. He could almost hear the voices of all the generations of suon of this line, and of his family, imprinted in the smallest measures of material in the fabric of the cuff.

Telling worlds. Witness to a promise he hadn't been given the time to make.

THE CASEWORKER AND her pewter man didn't visit again until two weeks later. Sooly escorted him once more to the same meeting room soon after the sun had risen fully to day. Teasing shards of golden light fell along their walking path like insubstantial flagstones, taking on the shape of the narrow windows set in the walls. Close to freedom but nowhere near it at the same time. For months that had been the reminder.

Seated inside the ashen room were the recordkeeper and the Mazoön woman, but also his sister Ba'Suon, Sephihalé ele Prita.

Prita stood immediately and they pressed into each other's arms before he could take visual stock of her, or her of him. It didn't matter. The flood of her presence buoyed him. Her rough embrace penetrated past the pressure of the caul and felt familiar and true. He shut his eyes against the stares of the Mazoön woman and the skeletal recordkeeper, and touched the back of his sister's head where the shorn stubble of her hair scratched his palm. Prita smelled of tanned hide and smoke, the opposite of this stone prison. His fingers slid and curled into the velvet texture of buckskin along her back. The hard weave of suon scales pressed against his chest, through the thin denim of the coveralls the Mazoön made him wear. These were all elements of his home.

Prita leaned back to kiss his face, to hold his face between her calloused palms. Her thumbs traced the rough texture of his sparse beard, something more Kattakan than Ba'Suon. When he looked at her, she was searching into him with amber eyes mixed with both relief and concern.

"You've been bleached like bone," she said.

His eyes began to fill. They were the color of shallow emerald waters now and would be strange to her, as their last sight of each other had been many years ago as youths. When he had first joined the Kattakan army, whole. "The war," he said.

She nodded without asking for more explanation and slipped her hands down to grasp his own in both of hers. She turned to the caseworker. "Can I take him with me?"

The woman pointed her chin to the table. "He needs to sign these papers. He refused until you were here."

It sounded like accusation.

Prita looked at him.

"I don't know what it says."

"I explained to him," said the woman.

Prita sat at the table and he followed. She put her hand out and the woman passed her the folder. For some time his sister read the Mazoön print. The caseworker breathed out audibly. Finally Prita met his eyes again. "It's all right. You can sign it. It says I will be responsible for you for a period of a year, and that one of their people will meet you to gauge your..." Something muted, but disgusted, flickered across her tanned features. "Behavior."

He switched to the short language known amongst their family, something the caseworker would not know. "She said I would be restricted. My knowing. There is some sort of Mazoön—" He waved his hand briefly. "It gouges at my mind here. Will I have to live with this?"

"Not forever. Not once you pass their probation. But they want me to report on what you do. I am restricted to some extent, even now. But it's not like this." She looked around the room, but she meant the prison. "You will see when we're on the land. Mostly they fear aggression, but in the course of our simple living, they can find no breaking of their laws." His sister paused and she touched his hand as it sat on the table. "They fear our communion with the suon, but we have no cause to be destructive. It will take time to show them, that's all."

"We're waiting," the caseworker said, a tightness to her eyes and mouth as she tried to glean some understanding of their conversation.

He picked up the pen from in front of the woman. He had fled a war and its army. He had no reason to be aggressive now, whether they believed him or not. So he made his mark on the papers. The metal man coughed and spat a block of paper from its mouth. The caseworker tore it free, removed some sticky surface layer and slapped it onto the corner of the sheet whereon he'd made his mark. The Mazoön symbol of a white chrysanthemum, bordered in gold, embossed the agreement of his release. Words circled the flower that he could not read. The caseworker nodded, satisfied.

"By order of the State Department of Mazemoor, you are free to go, Sephihalé ele Janan."

The recordkeeper burped. Its blank stare and glowing gold mouth seemed to agree.

THERE WERE A series of rooms into which he had to go before Prita could take him from this prison. Outside the meeting room, Prita kissed him and said she would wait for him at the exit, and he suffered a moment of doubt that these Mazoön would follow through on his release. He watched another guard escort Prita down the corridor before Sooly took hold of his arm to lead him in the opposite direction.

A woman inside a caged room gave over the clothes

in which he'd arrived in Mazemoor, along with his other belongings. They were folded in a brown paper bag with his harwa and gun, his boots on top. She passed his rifle and canteen through the gap beneath the barred window, then his medicines still in their suon scale cross-bag. For the last items—his twin blades made of suon bone, snug in the leather belt— she paused and examined them. Wrapped her hand around the hilt and pulled one free to angle the bone blade to the light. She made a sound of evaluation, looked at him as if such fine craftsmanship should not belong to him, then snapped the blade back in its sheath and passed through the whole belt. He took it and hung it over his shoulder and turned that shoulder to her. His arms full, he followed Sooly to a room nearby and Sooly told him to get dressed and to leave the coveralls inside, as if he'd want to take them with him.

Once the door shut for his privacy, he set his belongings on the long bench and checked his weapons. Both the gun and the rifle had no ammunition. He put them aside on the bench and for a moment stood breathing, staring at the white-painted brick wall. "Lilley, we're leaving." His voice sounded tinny in the dead air, his own language like a foreign tongue. Nothing answered back, not even a whisper. The weight built behind his eyes, but it wasn't from the prison.

He changed clothes. As piece by piece of his Ba'Suon attire became a part of himself again he began to breathe easier despite the compression of the caul. His tunic and trousers, made of golden elk skins, rubbed smooth against his body and smelled of woodsmoke and green air from the last camp he'd made before coming to this country. The copper-color suon scales stitched into the torso and sleeves, in the pattern of his family, made chime music as he belted on the holsters for both his gun and blades. Such subtle reminders of his life before this prison trickled memories back to him as through a sieve of the cold present. Lilley's hand tracing the smooth scales in the sun. At other times, wiping off someone else's blood. Or his own.

"Keep going," he said, as if to the absent man. How often had they pushed each other in such ways when flinging themselves away from a skirmish lost, the scent of Mazoön cannon fire still clinging to their clothes and burning the lining of their mouths?

He continued to adorn himself in his old clothes, watching his hands work like they were someone else's, in this room full of strange angles meant to discourage any lingering. His feet felt warm once again inside the felt-lined leather boots. When he hung the medicine bag across his chest and slipped the harwa on his wrist, an unbidden surge of tears battered behind his eyes. He wrapped his fingers around the cuff, but he still couldn't feel if Lilley were dead or alive. *Get on with it,* he could imagine Lilley saying. *Lallygag.*

He drew a deep breath and felt some ringing of his ancestral blood and the blood of the suon entwined with the harwa, and that truth spun a tranquil cocoon in the center of his chest. Done. He rubbed the heel of his palm across his shut lids, gathered up his rifle and canteen, and left behind the coveralls and paper bag dropped on the stone floor.

Sooly stared at him for a heavy moment as if seeing him for the first time. The prison's caul pulsed in his ears. He looked back with a directness he hadn't exercised through his imprisonment. Without touching, the guard gestured him to the barred window beneath which the woman passed him yet another piece of paper and a pen and told him to sign his name to show that he had received all of his possessions from the prison. He made his mark. She then handed him a small card with Mazoön writing on it and said to show this chit to the aviary administrator if he wanted the return of his 'dragon.'

When he spied Prita standing just inside the tall exterior gate of the prison, the sun falling around her shoulders without obstruction, he rushed forward, barely hearing the heavy clang of the door shutting definitively behind him.

She locked her arms around his waist and pressed her cheek to his shoulder. For a long moment they stood there together and her relief kissed his own. A knowing older than this city and its mythicism. A depth beyond blood. "Janan, devisha. Let's go and free your suon."

HE'D ARRIVED BY train to the city of Té'er, from the Mazoön coastal detention center that had caught him in his flight south. His wrists shackled, his suon confiscated, and their mythicism binding him solid, a weight upon his awareness. Nobody had wanted to answer his questions but he understood some truths from fighting these people in war. They relied on their mythicism for their strength and power, but it wasn't boundless. They could not stray too far from their lands, which had saved Kattaka from deep invasion, but their ways proved to be a steadfast and persistent defense. Yet the intricacies of their world beyond war remained a mystery. The train itself had felt like sitting inside a racketing snake, skeletal and predatory, as it slithered its way south on an iron-shod belly.

The ferry that took them to the island whereon Tourmaline was kept offered him a view of Té'er's eastern coastline. A handful of passengers in pressed, tight-fitting Mazoön garb gave them a wide berth, either seated on the wooden benches inside the wide cabin or lined along the deck rails. He and Prita in their animal skins and suon scales. He leaned against the aft rail beside his sister and she pointed out the black spires that bristled around the capital city of Mazemoor, a crown of thorns as a backdrop to the plethora of gilded rotundas, mosaic arches, and winged blue-tiled rooftops. "That is the mechanism of it all," she said.

"Mechanism?" He didn't know that word, the feel of it like a rock on his tongue amidst the common language of their people.

She spat down into the roiling gray sea and churning white foam in the ferry's wake. "The structure upon which they've built their civilization."

"I saw something similar on their northern coast. It caught me in my flight. Similar edifices stab the land through the city, especially the public places like the train station." Being near these narrow black silos gave him the same feeling as being imprisoned, surrounded on all sides by stone and iron, a shackle at the throat of nature. An unnatural state. Even from a little distance he'd noticed words and symbols engraved in the exterior panels, and it had seemed like the letters themselves could look at him. Or look through him.

"It's how they fuel their cities," Prita said. "How they grow their crops to aberrant abundance. How they order their 'mythicism.' They draw from the land and keep the elements in those towers."

"The elements of the land?"

"It's so."

"But... how?"

"I don't know precisely. But the words they've formed out of existence, the bastardization of their ancient knowing... it's somehow to do with that." Her finger slid across the horizon. "See those black and gray marks? The chalk-white streaks on the waterfront? All of this used to be green shore and pearl rock. And the water used to be blue."

"I don't understand."

His sister in the family looked up at him, her arms braced on the brass rail of the chugging vessel. Behind them, the Mazoön language murmured as if telling secrets. The island on which they kept Tourmaline was, apparently, some sort of holiday destination. Their presence seemed to sour that.

Prita said, "Beyond their fear of our communion with the suon is their distrust of our innate understanding of the world and the cosmos. They don't know what can't be named, so they intend to bind everything in the confines of their concepts. And thus move the mountains."

He regarded the steadily receding, ravaged shoreline of the great city of Té'er. Built by their common ancestors, but long after both Ba'Suon and Ma'Suon had once gathered as a convocation of families. Long after the Mazoön—what now they called themselves—had expelled his people from this island. *Keep going.*

He wrapped his hand around the harwa on his wrist, and held on.

THE AVIARY SAT upon the tallest hill on the island, skirted by vaulting trees and thick blue bush. From the lower shore all Janan saw was the dome's iron spike at its peak. The climb to the administrative center required scaling stone and wooden steps embedded in the hillside through the shadowed trees, accessible just a hundred feet from the ferry dock. They weren't the only ones making the trek; an eel line extended behind them as a couple dozen holidaying Mazoön with parasols and boxy hats followed them like they were all on a pilgrimage to some sacred site.

At the top was a plateau of excavated gray stone,

surrounded by the trees that hadn't been hewed away, and in the heart of the plateau stood a sprawling wooden building with a peaked roof and two doors on opposite ends. One sign painted in bold yellow Mazoön script said *Visitors' Entrance*, Prita translated. The other door was labeled *Administration*. They departed the line of well-dressed Mazoön to head toward the administrative portico and were halted by an indigo-uniformed guard similar to what Janan had encountered in the northern detention center.

The woman said something in the Mazoön tongue. Prita answered likewise, and the guard looked at Janan from head to toe. She gestured with two gloved fingers at his face and Prita said something else. Janan held his empty rifle and watched the Mazoön's pinched, dark eyes. Prita spoke again and the guard answered briskly before she turned and disappeared inside the building.

Prita looked at him. "She's going to talk to her superior."

"What did you say?"

"That you were here to collect your suon from the aviary."

"She seemed to take issue with my appearance."

"She didn't believe you were Ba'Suon."

The guard appeared again and motioned them inside. Janan followed his sister into some sort of office space, a couple of desks and colorful maps on the wall of what Janan gleaned to be the topography of Mazemoor and its child islands. The guard disappeared behind a door.

Another uniformed individual sat at one of the desks, scratching in a notebook. He didn't acknowledge them, as if their mere presence was sufficient reason to reinforce how little he thought of their existence. Janan and Prita waited, and after some minutes and a slight flourish as he made his mark upon the paper, the young man looked up. He asked a question and Prita answered. It sounded like the same words from outside. The guard touched some sort of metal box on his desk and spoke to it. As his words hit the surface it glowed the same gold that Janan had seen in the recordkeeper's mouth. After a short while, an older woman appeared through one of the rear doors. The buttons on her indigo uniform glinted like cat eyes, her cap festooned with gold braiding. An officer of her people. She looked at both Prita and Janan, scrutinized their clothes, and settled her gaze on Janan.

She spoke haltingly in their language. "I help you?"

Before Prita could speak, Janan stepped forward and produced the chit from his medicine bag.

The woman accepted it and read it front and back. She nodded and said something to the young man at the desk, then motioned to them to follow her through the rear door, where they passed an inner room lined with more desks and half a dozen other uniforms. All of them were about some industrious tasks that required paper and metal boxes. As he and Prita walked through, one by one the Mazoön eyes lifted and regarded them with somber surprise. Their boots sounded heavy on the wood plank floor. The officer led them right through an exterior door, down steps onto gravel and across a stone path leading into the bush.

They climbed a rough-hewn path marked by weathered stairs like a trail of broken teeth through the mouth of the trees. The further they went, the louder became the cries of the suon trapped in the iron aviary, and Janan began to feel the agitation of this imprisonment bearing down on the back of his shoulders. He counted at least five suon voices, chief among them Tourmaline, and tried to step past the officer to hurry this process, but she said something sharp at his back.

Prita said, "Wait, devisha."

He looked back. The Mazoön woman gestured with one hand, the other on the gun at her hip. He slowed, and she passed him. He didn't need language to understand the look in her eyes, that he should mind his place. He bit the inside of his cheek to remind himself of necessary pain, the kind that led to greater freedoms, if such a word could be used in this land. The officer forced their pace in the slow ascent until finally they broke the upper treeline onto a small platform embedded into the cliffside. Upon it stood another administrative building, smaller. Janan bypassed it and headed for the base of the towering iron cage.

"Stop him!" Followed by another command in the Mazoön tongue.

Prita caught up and seized his arm. "Janan. Wait.

They have a way of doing things here."

"I can hear her." Tourmaline. Anxious and rippling fear and anger toward him. *i in teeth and crush in bone* He heard the smaller suon in the cage too, a fainter distress.

Two guards appeared from the building, armed. Janan looked at them, at the officer in her rigid uniform, sweat now beaded on her skin from the climb.

"Let them do things in order," Prita murmured to him.

The officer said something to Prita and pointed to the building and the broad deck extending out from its porch, grounded into the mountain. Prita took him to it to wait. The officer talked to the guards and soon they disappeared toward the aviary.

"Your dragon comes," said the officer.

Janan cast his gaze to the sky, the dome of blue and the hair-wisp clouds feathered on its face. He knew the moment his suon was released when a rush of sunlight flared behind his eyes and the resonant bellow of Tourmaline's call echoed untrammeled through the trees. She came to him as a blinding shard of gold and coronal white, her expanded wings casting shadow over the widest edges of the mountain. He called to her in ululation, lifting his fist as she soared and circled above their heads.

i and sun and fire in air

The Mazoön all huddled near their building. The black spires on the north and south borders that Janan now noticed pointing toward the sky glowed forge-red as Tourmaline began her descent toward him. Gusts of wind stirred the scales on his clothes and created soft music in response to the thunderous, layered whistling coursing through her armor.

The platform on which he and Prita stood shook with the impact of the suon's legs as she alighted and settled, slowly folding her wings back and casting her javelin-sharp muzzle toward the sky. She blew, nostrils flared and ears back, and the scent of earthen smoke permeated the atmosphere around them all. Janan stepped forward into the fall of her shadow and placed the flat of his palm along the base of her throat to slowly rub the gold paneling. The light glinting off it made him squint. He murmured to her in their language, bombarded with *goldshard* and *bloodred* from her creature thoughts. The latter was her way of asking after Lilley. Beneath it, a strange susurration he did not recognize.

He pressed his cheek to her heaving chest, where scars of flesh showed beneath thin lines of missing scale, and listened to the deep resounding of her heart instead, his own a smaller echo through his ears. Her head curved down, nose nudging his shoulder until he looked up to meet the burning gold of her eye. A jagged scar cut through her left and cast that eye in milky white, but the clear one blazed. *i in fire and blood and brother*

"He's not here," he said. She stared at him for a long moment then tossed her chin up and bellowed. The

Mazoön covered their ears. Tourmaline's tapered left ear twitched, and Janan saw the black stud pierced through its base. He looked at the Mazoön standing in their protective circle. "What is that?"

The officer spoke and Prita translated to him. "It's so we can track her. We are relying on you to control her, as per your agreement with State, but should she run rogue we will also know it and we will hunt her down. Should you remove it, we'll know that too, and consider it a violation of your agreement."

Prita touched his arm to stay his response, catching the look in his eyes. And probably feeling the tension in his body. "We understand." She said to him in their Ba'Suon tongue: "Let's go. It's a long journey to home."

"Shorter if we fly."

"We can't. Not from inside the city borders."

"Will I have to walk my suon the entire distance?"

"No, she can follow us from the air. Make her understand. It's for our safety, and hers."

A part of him wanted to test the boundaries of this Mazoön mythicism. Their inscrutable black silos and heavy borders groping at his awareness like a trapper's hand, hoping to scurry the core of him into some metal box so they could seal him inside himself. They had done it to his suon also, but Tourmaline had spent enough time in cages; so had he. So he remained silent.

They made him sign another piece of paper verifying that his suon was unharmed and released to him. He wondered where all these pieces of scribbling went, imagined a room the size of this mountain filled by thin sheets spilled from the open mouths of metal men. He handed back the board and pen to the officer, and she and her guards disappeared inside their wooden building. Janan looked up at Tourmaline and roughly stroked her muzzle as she dipped to meet his touch, the rumble of pleasure rolling through the high air like the reverberations of an earthquake. The color blue passed between them but instead of climbing onto her back, as she expected, he walked along her flank and rubbed his hand down the spine of her left wing. She was free and she could follow. When she curved her long neck to look back at him, he lifted his fist into the air once more and stepped back off the stone platform.

She launched herself toward the thin clouds, calling to the sky. The trapped suon still in the aviary echoed back her cries.

Prita's spread was far outside Té'er and so they rode the train, his second encounter with the beast. The glut of city citizens with their tall hats and tight clothing seemed endless in the winding walk from the carriage that took them from the gull-infested ferry dock to the interior ticket window. The station's vaulted hall echoed with the sound of the population from mosaic ceiling to tiled floor, where hurried footsteps tapped a rhythm from one platform to the next. People still walked wide of them and a few children exclaimed and pointed. Nobody else wore weapons and this seemed the crux of the Mazoön distress, but Prita said that should any officers of the law stop them, he had his papers and she also had papers that deemed it legal, as his guns were unloaded and the blades were a recognized part of Ba'Suon culture. He made no comment all the way to the train that would head southwest, seeing instead the turquoise blue sky and his suon circling beneath it, waiting on them. Even free, however, the touch of her presence seemed wrapped in a skein from which neither of them could disentangle. Their mutual agitation at this foreign reality sounded between them like the hiss of a thousand tongues.

He managed to convince Tourmaline to remain aloft and follow him along the track, imagining the clear skies and cold air that she craved, regardless of their trepidation and an undercurrent of nervousness at this speeding enclosure in which he was trapped. For her own sake, his suon had to fly high enough not to disturb the passengers or alert the projectile weapons of defense lined around the borders of the city. But so high and only faint ripples trickled to him of her presence.

In the rattling car somewhere in the mid-belly position of the steel serpent, he and Prita sat across from each other on either side of a polished wooden table. The interior of the train was like sitting in a Kattakan house, an experience of which he knew only a little and had no desire to repeat: the straight lines, unnatural glass lighting, and static, garish paintings on the walls, of ancestors trapped in their own image. The train bore the same aesthetics, though at least lacked the eyes of the dead.

The Mazoön passengers around them in their high collars and layered frocks, the women unnaturally sleeked in colorful patterns of silk and brocade, spoke in hushed voices at first, glancing their way, though the Mazoön didn't have to fear since he couldn't understand a word they said, nor did he care. He wasn't shackled for this venture, and he wasn't headed to some city prison, but as the day fled by at the rate of the rolling green vista outside the windows, he felt no more reassured. Even with Prita's promise that they would not be obstructed on their journey, he couldn't quite be convinced.

So she tried to distract him with conversation in their familial language, something the people around them wouldn't understand.

"Tell me how this happened." She passed her palm down over her face to indicate his appearance.

It was a natural question, but speaking the words would take him to the time and there was enough pain in his thoughts as his own semblance of freedom reminded him of what he lacked. What he'd left back in the Kattakan-occupied lands. His fingers hooked through his harwa and tugged.

"You said the war," his sister prompted.

"Their mythicism." He glanced at the Mazoön around them.

"How?"

"I don't know. Maybe in the same way they tear the elements from the land. Something in their mythicism also tore something from me." The wildflower honey of his eyes and complexion. The walnut brown of his hair. The way Lilley had named these colors in him with affectionate specificity, a romanticism Janan teased him about—only for the Mazoön to shock them away. His body remembered the impact and the way he and Tourmaline had fallen from the sky into the long waters. That battle had also taken Lilley's left hand. Mythicism and dragonshot, both of them riding into the assault in defense of a land in which they could not live freely. He stared out the window at features that seemed familiar but raced by too quickly for him to know or recall. His ancestors had traveled these paths.

Beneath this train, the golden glow of the tracks touched the blur of ground. What was being drained in order for this machine to run?

He looked back at Prita, who watched him with the patience of a fox. "How is it you own Mazoön land?"

She leaned back with a pull of breath. "It's not the best land, but it is land and it's mine. When I first came here, I cooperated with them. I told them everything I knew about the Kattakan forces. Sometimes I flew back to the north isle to gather more information for them. When the war ended, they parceled me the land." She turned her palms up on the table. "There is no satisfaction in how it came to me, but at least it's mine."

"I wish I'd done the same." From the first season he'd met Lilley. If they'd fled instead of fought.

"Sometimes I wonder," said Prita.

He met her eyes. "What?"

"If it wouldn't have been better to stay and gather together. If all of the families had gathered together against the Kattakans and allied with the Mazoön. Our ancestral families had once been one people, after all, when the Mazoön were our cousin Ma'Suon. We could have pressed out the invaders."

"Or been completely destroyed. Even without any kind of knowing, or mythicism, the Kattakans are powerful in their skills." In the ingenuity of their weaponry. In their conquering spirit. "At the time the Mazoön wanted nothing to do with the north either. Not until they were threatened."

"We will never know, I suppose. The land is preserved?"

Ba'Suon land. For a moment the ache in his heart pierced sharply. "Beyond the towns and the city of Diam that they built. But the Kattakans grow and spread."

"Like a rash," she said.

He looked back out the window. The landscape didn't seem to change, only cycled as though a ribbon of it surrounded the entire train and was merely pulled along in a great, unending circle.

THE TO AND fro of the train's going rocked him into an uneasy slumber. He was only able to allow himself to do it because his sister remained awake. Though his dreams had followed him into this foreign land, they consisted of the same shadows. The sound of the angling cannons and winding guns as Tourmaline circled Fort Nemiha overhead, calling for him. The Kattakan soldiers tearing back the door of the tent wherein he and Lilley slept, the hard hands that yanked them apart and flung them to the ground. Abhvihin ele Raka standing behind Lord Shearoji's shoulder, holding the stolen harwa between his fingers. They were dreams, not memories. Not precisely. But the images did not matter as much as the emotion, and in his dreams he raged.

Opening his eyes in muddled intervals, he began to note a pattern on this blazing Mazoön landscape, though it took some stretch of time for him to puzzle it together from the weary shards of his attention.

"I saw those silos in the north country. At the borders of the long waters. They're truly everywhere here."

He spoke quietly but Prita heard immediately over the whir and grind of the train's progress. She leaned forward to touch his wrist as his arm lay on the table between them.

"Like the spikes in Té'er," she said.

But these wilderness silos seemed roughly wrought and they appeared moments before the train stopped at any town. On the land in between, only sparse construction. Once or twice, as he gazed out at the russet scape, he recalled through his doze passing arrow-like windmills protruding from the earth, whipped by the natural forces of the world. In other flashes, those same black spires as in Té'er, motionless and engraved. Towering silos of mythicism that somehow captured the essence of the world in their words. The land here—unlike at Té'er—spread cracked and barren, with low yellow grass and distant red plateaus. Here and there, spidery trees with thin, fanned leaves sprouted in clusters.

The train fumed to a slothful halt. More awake, he watched as the Mazoön passengers shuffled down the aisle, pulling cases from racks overhead to disembark at the station. People, children, a couple of dogs, a woman carrying a cage wherein a bright orange bird fluttered. Outside stood a long platform with a dark interior housing he couldn't penetrate with his naked gaze. The train whistled and began its slow slither forward once more. Beyond the station there was a half-cobbled road in a bleach-boarded town of tiled roofs and long clay walls. Sprouting above it all was a ring of those tall black spires.

"I can feel them," he said. The throbbing insistence behind his eyes.

"You seem particularly sensitive to their effect," his sister said. "Maybe I've grown too used to them. These Mazoön desire to rule all the land with those silos, no matter how far-flung, drilling down to the bowels of the earth or reaching into the fingers of the wind to seize what they can from its grip."

"But is that the entirety of what they do? Are they intent only on plunder?"

She shrugged. "In the cities they provide physical care through this power. But I have never seen it. What are we to do about it, either way?" She gestured up to the sky in the manner of their people: *as the stars deem it*. "We're the next stop."

The closest village to Prita's land was called Wister, named after the founder Eben Wisterel, who bred suon, she said. The businesses sprang up to support this 'dragon baron' and his crew. He supplied many of the suon to surrounding villages and towns and even as far as Heron Lake, the nearest large city to the west. Prita said the Mazoön who bred suon were not like the Ba'Suon who bred suon for their families, only enough to strengthen a crown and support life on the land. Breeding suon in Mazemoor was an industry. He was beginning to understand fully the driven shape of this country and none of it had much in common with their mutual ancestry.

Prita led him from the train station's simple wooden platform to the dirt channel leading to the village proper. Though the way was smooth in the sunshine, he could see the muddy path it would become in wetter weather. Further up a gentle incline were a handful of squat wooden buildings, neatly cut but with shutters missing here and there, roof tiles fallen, a certain unkemptness to the fencing and raggedy edges of the awnings. Roughshod metal columns supported the taller buildings—scaffolding for repairs, though only a handful of workers seemed at the task. The road was cobbled haphazardly with pale desert rocks of various sizes, which petered out along the edges. There were hitching posts for horses and iron perches for suon—the latter surprised him. They were too small for Tourmaline but as his gaze raked the sky he spied a dozen diminutive breeds whirling like vultures above the village. Just on the borders, those same black spires, but only two. One looked a little tilted, as if a giant had leaned on it.

The small suon cawed and suddenly broke away, disappearing toward the edges of the village. A couple landed in the shadow of the general store's awning, making a line of white lanterns flit. Above, Tourmaline's resonant scale-song tore through the heavens like a hurricane wind and all the people looked up in alarm as the battle suon dove to the middle of the street. Janan stepped forward to meet her landing even as folks exclaimed and ran, seeking refuge inside the buildings until only he and his suon occupied the road. Under the early evening light, Tourmaline's scales glinted and rippled with gold and blue. Her fanning wings cast the empty center of the village square into dusk. A well bucket from some previous era swung creaking from the breeze of it.

"You didn't like the flight," he murmured to her, putting out his hand for her muzzle to graze. She felt the stud in her ear like he felt it too, even free of the prison's caul. Some kind of buzzing, a low and consistent rub of headache behind his eyes that muffled all of nature. Reminding them both of their tethering. He felt the frustration in the way she blew and how her tail snapped from side to side, its arrow point cutting the air like a scythe, like there was an enemy in their vicinity. A dog some distance down the street barked furiously.

Prita said behind him, "Everyone knows you've arrived now. Come."

He turned to see his sister holding the halter rein of a crimson suon, obsidian black around its muzzle and on the tips of its crest, fanned high and alert now. A male, only half the size of Tourmaline as these southern suon seemed to be, but with deep orange eyes like two flames that danced in Tourmaline's direction. He must have been one of the suon flying above, waiting for Prita. The suon's neck stretched so he could sniff Tourmaline's hindquarters but she flicked her left wing in warning. Janan stepped on her foreleg and swung himself onto her back. They launched toward the clouds and when he looked down at the sudden distance of the village below, now so small it appeared to be a collection of child's toys, he spied the slow trickle of people emerging from their shelters. Prita joined him in the air on the back of her suon and they winged west into the darkening bloody edges of the sky.

HER SPREAD WAS a single house after the fashion of the Mazoön, with a barn large enough to house Tourmaline, a single aviary which was the largest structure by far on the plot, and a corral for the couple of horses kept apart from the suon. In every direction lay desert, bracken and scrub and, intermittently, those squat trees he'd seen on the land during their travel, wide fat leaves on narrow bone-white stalks like spirits rooted to the earth in the afterlife. In the distance, the thin silhouette of the village of Wister and its numerous tiny lights like spider eyes set against a falling sky. The black silos that Prita said gave the populace its 'energy' were like ancient needles boring holes in the heavens through which the stars shone, or else the stars were the holes themselves, revelators of some arching, all-encompassing crystal dome.

The aviary door stood open and Prita released her suon to it, where he flew in to join the crown of four other desert suon nested within. She looked up at Janan as he stepped down from Tourmaline's back. "She can hunt. There are wolves in the area, wild bulls that might be more her game. A herd of plateau goats on the southern ridge. The Mazoön populate the land with game for the suon they might introduce to these areas to keep the world in balance, so at least they are aware. But I'm certain there is no other suon of Tourmaline's size or temperament in the whole region. We'll have to keep an eye on her hunting. That's part of the condition of your release."

He nodded, hefting his pack and the rifle on his shoulder. It was the most fundamental imperative of their people. If the suon overpopulated a region, the Ba'Suon gathered them, or else all the wildlife and the land suffered. Northern suon, at least, could live for centuries and impacted the land over long periods of time if their migratory patterns were disrupted like they had been from the war in what was now Eastern Kattaka. It seemed Mazemoor did not forget all of its ancient teachings and minded the population of their wild suon.

He watched as Tourmaline walked a crescent around the spread, stopped and pissed her dominance into the dirt. The sharp metallic scent of it permeated the air. She bellowed, a declaration to all creatures in the area. The desert suon in the aviary clung to the iron bars and cawed back. Tourmaline ignored them and swung her tail high and looked at him. *i and thorn and sky* He approached and stroked his hand down her flank, a brief feeling of caution and restraint. A muddle of memory from the aviary up north passed through him like a cold wind and he showed her the prison cell in which he'd slept all those days and nights. She fanned her wings at him and took a step forward. She understood the danger of this land and their need to watch, so arrowed herself back into the sky for the hunt. Dust hung in the air long after she pasted into the clouds. Flight would soothe her even if it could not eliminate the discomfort of the Mazoön mythicism that peppered them both like a ceaseless rattle.

He went to the aviary to meet the smaller cousins of this spread. Turquoise, silver, rose, and spring green suon. Some secondary coloring on all of them—tips of the muzzle and ears, ends of the tail, around the thick haunches. All were young, all were female besides the crimson, judging from the shape of their brows, no more than twenty years. They flitted from iron bar to iron bar, greeting him with trills and the occasional flick of their tails. Their presence danced in the center of his chest like playful music. Happy but a little nervous at his new scent, at the battle suon he brought with him. He held his hand through the bars and the crimson-obsidian suon hopped over to gently sniff up his arm. He waited for the long ashen tongue to dart out and taste his hand, where it left behind a clear viscous liquid that protected its mouth from fire. He rubbed along its throat where the red paneling shone like garnets and a soft nudge of *redsun* drifted to him in memory, nothing more. The ghost of his harwan stirred by the gentle commingling of suon curiosity with his own. Lilley possessed a strange affinity for the creatures and often Janan had watched him speak to the suon in the clumsy manner of a Kattakan, bestowing on them fanciful names. *You know they don't use language like you do*, he'd said to Lilley. To which Lilley had replied, *It don't matter, so long as they understand.* They'd shared a smile and Lilley said, *Kinda like you. Didja need to understand my language to know I wanted to kiss ya?*

"Come inside," Prita said, standing on the porch. Her voice pulled apart the gossamer strands of his memory and released them to the stars. She smiled at him, at the sight of him with the suon. He saw light glowing through the square windows of the house. The structure was foreign but the warmth, at least, was familiar.

No mythicism silos on Prita's spread; candle and lamp flame greeted him. It appeared to be all one room like a mata, but strangely divided—Kattakan and perhaps Mazoön influence with the hearth to one side instead of in the center, a couple of beds cordoned by a hanging sheet of felt, shelves mostly shadowed so he couldn't quite make out their contents beyond pots and jars. A plainly wrought table and four chairs of all different design, and a second door on the opposite wall that perhaps led to another room or to the outside. Everything was unadorned, lacking the vibrant colors and ancestral markings of the Ba'Suon, nothing here to reflect the cosmos or tradition. Except for the honor table in the corner, lit by candles and festooned with beading, necklaces made of suon scales, and intricate embroidery on swatches of cotton in the pattern of the stars. Tokens for the dead. Despite the light and the cook stove, a cold ran through him.

"I had thought you'd erect a mata," he said.

Prita said, "No." She gestured to a young man sitting by the iron stove, in shadow. "This is Sephihalé ele Omala. My son."

The boy straightened to his feet, shoulders back in a stance of vague challenge. He seemed almost the age Janan had been when he'd joined the war fifteen years ago, not quite an adult stature. Not blooded in the least. Slight of build. In the dim light his hair captured reddish-gold tones, his eyes the black of an eclipse. A strong resemblance to his mother and tendrils of somebody else. Janan nodded to him and spoke his own name.

48

"You're my uncle," the boy said.

"Older brother." He cast a look Prita's way. "Your mother and I aren't blood-related, but we're of the same family." So she hadn't taught her son the organization of their people. Perhaps she hadn't any need, considering they might be the only Ba'Suon in the region.

"Why are you so pale?"

"That's a story for later, perhaps," Prita said, already moving to a basin to wash her hands and face. "Get food on the table, it smells good and we're hungry."

He felt how his presence changed the air in this space to something quite thin, like Kattakan reliquary glass. The wrong breath might crack the congeniality thrust between them. The young man was unsure of him but deeply curious. It came off him like scent. Prita occupied herself, but all of her attention, even without a direct gaze, felt sharp to his ears and against his skin. She was sounding the way he and her son moved. Janan removed his boots by the door and leaned his belongings with them. The boy watched him, gaze lingering on the weapons, his guns and blades that he carefully lay on the bench against the wall. Prita hadn't removed her boots. The reverberations of her stepping back and forth across the plank floor echoed heavily. He emptied the same basin in the sink and rinsed it with jug water, filled it again and washed his hands and face. The water was tepid but clean. Behind him, he heard his sister and Omala setting the table and the fragrant scent of meat stew and floral tea wafted from the stove.

"Is it just you two?" he asked as they ate. The boy sat across from him and stared openly.

Prita sipped her tea. She glanced toward the honor table. "It's so. Omala's father died some years ago."

"From what family was he?"

"Mazoön," she said.

He tried not to be surprised, and after a moment of consideration, wasn't. He had no idea what the years had been like for her, beyond the sketches she'd drawn for him in brief conversation.

"Do you have someone?" Her gaze found the harwa around his wrist. "You touch it often."

"In Kattaka."

She nodded like she understood. But Omala said, "Why didn't they come with you?" It wasn't curiosity, but confrontation. Suspicion.

He spooned the stew and filled his mouth. The boy's lips twisted in subtle judgment, as if the lack of answer confirmed something in his mind.

"Where's your suon?" he asked his sister. The crown outside were of this land, not from a gather in the north.

"He died in battle," she said. "But from Kattakan artillery. They said it was an accident but that's when I came to Mazemoor."

From the hardness in her eyes, he understood. Such an anger would never quite die.

After washing the dishes, he sat on the porch and struck a match for his Fortune cigarette and smoked. He watched the dark and the deep shadows that crept to the porch once the light from the house dissipated across the ground. Insects wrought a chiming tune. The moon played coy, half-obscured by a smudge of clouds. Tourmaline hadn't returned and the homestead suon rumbled only faintly as they slept. The two horses nickered and swished their tails but otherwise remained motionless. All the world abed, as peaceful as a camp of their people. Fatigue weighed on him, but he breathed the dry, slightly acrid air, like the dregs of a fire discarding its memory through him. The door slid open behind him and Prita joined him on the step. She puffed on a long wooden pipe. Ba'Suon engravings adorned the bowl, the swirls of the cosmos with a suon dancing in its coils.

"What happened here?" he asked.

"Omala's father built this spread. I've thought about tearing it down and putting up a mata, but it's all he's known. I suppose after years, I got used to it. Like I've become used to this country and its ways." She looked at him through the smoke and its faint scent of apple blossom. A scent of home. "I'm so happy you're here, devisha. It's been lonely for very long."

He flicked his ashes onto the dirt and leaned his shoulder against hers. "Didn't you find others? They must be here. The caseworker mentioned."

"I see them occasionally. The ones that live in families on the land. The ones in the cities... they are different. But this is the land I was given and once I was with Hetram, we were content together."

He thought of the military camps in which he and

Lilley had bided their time. Where they'd met. And later, with Raka. The three of them as a unit that worked well on the battlefield. For a while it had felt like that was all they needed. Not the loving chaos of a family and definitely not the chaos of army life. In the midst of war they'd carved somewhere in between, a staying place far-flung from regular paths because his path had not been the same as his family's for many years. A frontier of their own rhythms and a certain desperate solitude. But the army, and Raka, hadn't allowed that to continue. Maybe Prita had just as much reason to divorce herself to this land, with her Mazoön harwan, a shared dream like the dreams he and Lilley had shared of flying south. A freedom of their own making.

"You must miss him," he said. His own heart pulsed with the strength and pain of rage. The rage of distance, of forced separation. Something akin to death. "Your Hetram."

"I do. As you must. What is their name?"

"Lilley. His own people kept him and his family as servants. He loves the land as we do."

"If Tourmaline didn't kill him, I assume he is of a good nature."

"She loves him too."

Prita exhaled her smoke. They looked at the night. The moon overhead like a blind eye. "You'll stay out here?"

"Until Tourmaline returns."

"I will share sleep with my son. You can have my

bed when you're ready. We'll fix a more permanent solution later." She stood, pressing her hand to his shoulder.

He touched it in acknowledgment before she returned inside. He heard her say something to Omala in Mazoön, foreign words in a foreign land, and rested his eyes on the horizon's brocade of stars, searching for his suon.

HE AWOKE AS if from a drowning, rising to the morning light like a spirit in new form. A gasp of disbelief that he could breathe. His body sunken into the bedding, his head heavy. Tendrils of his dream sought to hold him down in its oblivion, the echoes of an argument ringing in his ears momentarily louder than the Mazoön caul. He felt the day was sometime before noon and lay in the bed beneath Prita's woven blanket, listening to the sound of suon and horses outside. Occasionally, in the brief bouts of silence, chickens squawked and goats brayed. He recognized Tourmaline's bullying voice above it all and felt her agitation, but no reaching of his awareness could assuage it. She ignored him, and it forced him to sit up.

Outside, he leaned on the porch rail and sipped the coffee that had been left warming on the stove. He watched Omala rubbing down one of the small suon to clean its scales of dust and grime. Its paneling was a deep rose, like scar flesh. The others in the crown hopped and fluttered in play. Some distance away, beyond the horse corral, Tourmaline sat and stared at the eastern horizon, wings flicking occasionally. A sense of discomfort but without a source. She hadn't slept well either. When she felt him there, she swung her head around and looked at him with her one good eye, demanding.

"Yes," he said to her. Today they'd explore.

He washed himself head to toe outside behind a tall wooden screen built for the purpose. The last of the prison and the beard he shaved away sloughed with the dirty water he let spill to the stone embedded in the ground, where it ran off in a channel away from the property. After, Prita offered to braid his hair, so he sat below her on the porch steps and smoked as her fingers worked nimbly, partitioning the wet locks. He gave her the scales with which to cinch off the ends, some he'd carried from the north. They were Tourmaline's, gold and white, shed in autumn. Lilley used to do this for him, clumsily at first, then later one-handed and with his teeth, pulling the ends of his hair through the hollow of the scales. He smoked a little harder and squinted at the day. Sometimes Omala looked over from the aviary until it seemed his curiosity won, and he strode toward them to watch his mother.

The boy spoke haltingly in their language. "What're you doing?"

"Ba'Suon men," Prita said, "wear their hair like this."

This seemed to amuse her son, like her words were a quaint truth. "Why don't you grow your hair like that?"

Prita said, "Ba'Suon women do not. What did I tell you?"

"The tattoos on your scalp are open to the cosmos. Whatever that means."

"We receive its wisdom," she said.

"That means the men aren't wise?"

"Men are rarely wise," she said around the scales between her teeth. A teasing tone. "Remember that."

He considered the work his mother was doing, then leaned back and looked at Janan with an unimpressed flatness to his mouth.

"Your suon's real big."

"She's northern."

"They much bigger there?"

"Many are."

"Them scars're from the war?"

Janan nodded, watching the froth of questions rise in the boy's eyes. But they rang with a note of interrogation. The boldness of a young man with a need to assert himself.

"What was that like?" Omala said.

"Hsst," Prita said. A warning.

Janan flicked his ashes. "It's all right. The boy should know he's fortunate to have never touched battle." He tilted up his chin to regard the young face, burnished by sun and weather, the natural workings of the world. Nothing beyond that. The faint freckles across his nose reminded him of Lilley. Let the boy elbow his way into knowledge. "If you like, we can ask Tourmaline if she'd let you ride with me."

That lifted the boy's entire expression. Excitement thrummed from his chest but he dampened it with a glance of skepticism and guardedness. "Really?" A brief pause. "You name your suon."

"I didn't name her. My harwan did."

Omala looked at his mother. "I'm gonna name ours."

"No," Prita said, but there wasn't any weight to it. She pat Janan's shoulder to tell him she was finished and he stood, forcing the boy back a step.

With his hair in three braids down his neck and shoulders he felt the sun along his throat, face tilted up to receive the warmth. It almost off-set the Mazoön mote behind his eyes, the constant reminder that he had to account for himself in this land. That they would somehow know if he disobeyed their rules. He had thought being away from the prison would dismember the feeling, but it had only dimmed.

"Come." He dropped the remainder of his cigarette in the dirt. "If Tourmaline doesn't eat you immediately, she might tolerate you on her back."

The boy looked alarmed but Prita just laughed.

TOURMALINE REFUSED THE boy and barely abided Omala's rose suon to sniff at her hindquarters. None of the small crown approached beyond that or attempted to compete for territory by pissing over her mark, so the battle suon paid them little mind. She glanced at the boy and when Janan attempted to cajole her to allow Omala's touch, she blocked their way with a pointed fold of her wing.

i and redsun and sky
gold and cloud

She missed Lilley. She knew he did too. Janan stroked the velvet skin of her wing but she lifted it away and flicked her tail.

"Maybe later," he said to Omala. The boy's disappointment could have carved glass, but the simple introduction to the battle suon seemed to alleviate some of his initial hostility. His gaze lingered on her, squinting up as her head blocked the angle of the sun. Perhaps his awe outweighed his suspicion.

Janan armed his rifle and gun with ammunition he'd found on one of Prita's shelves. They mounted up with empty supply bags strapped to their suon—Prita rode the crimson and obsidian male once more—and flew to Wister when the sun was beginning to arc past high noon, a burning eye over the village. Tourmaline bellowed for the sheer joy of it, the deep bass of her flight a constant hum beneath the higher song of the smaller suon winging just below her. From this altitude he could see the long expanse of the russet land and a darker dotting of spider trees just beyond the wartish mark of the village. Red flats to the south. A herd of horses huddled on another spread in the southwest. And here and there, especially over Wister itself, the arrowed shapes of desert suon idling in the air.

They alighted just outside of Wister. Prita reckoned it would cause less ruckus if Tourmaline didn't chase the people indoors again. As long as she didn't harass the local suon while they bought their supplies, it would be a straightforward excursion. He took his rifle with him, slung along his back, and followed his sister and her son.

Regardless of his suon, they still drew stares. He supposed this was usual when any stranger appeared, and his evident strangeness was bound to garner curiosity beyond the familial interest of his young brother. The Mazoön noticed him with sharper attention. The women spoke behind fluttering fans and demure dips of their parasols, and the men in their straight edges and sculpted hats watched in rippling silence as they made their way from the center street to the general store.

A metal man resembling the recordkeeper greeted them just inside the door with its blank skull expression, though the round eyes immediately lit red, and an alarming grinding noise emanated from its face.

"Hey," said a woman behind the purchase counter. "No weapons in here."

He looked at Prita. She hadn't worn any, not even her blades, but she also hadn't warned him. He would have left the rifle behind but not his blades.

"I forgot," she murmured at his shoulder. "Best you wait outside."

"I'll come with you," Omala said, as if he needed a chaperone, but together they left the store and walked a little ways to a fenced enclosure wherein horses stood saddled and a couple of piebald hogs fed at a trough.

Janan leaned his back against the rails and lit a cigarette. Omala climbed up to sit on the top bar, hooking his ankles on the lower rungs, and held out his hand. For a few silent moments they shared the smoke like two Ba'Suon camp wranglers and watched the wary Mazoön pass by. The people looked at them while trying to hide the fact that they were looking at them.

"They got used to us," Omala said, "but you don't look like us, brother."

"What do people do here besides work?"

"You mean for entertainment? There's a parlor and dance hall. A community eatery. A tavern. We have seasonal festivals and sometimes troupes come through. You know, stage shows and acrobats." He dragged on the smoke. "There's an annual flight, a dragon race. Eben Wisterel sponsors that. People make lanterns and cook out. My mother won a couple years ago. There are bigger races in the cities like Té'er. I bet Tourmaline would win them all. You could make real coin."

"Do they have pit suon?"

"What's that?"

So the Mazoön weren't as barbaric as the Kattakans, it seemed. "My suon doesn't race." He nodded toward the thin black silos on the border. The odd one leaning as if it were some remnant of an older civilization. "Do you know how those work exactly?"

"The conduits?" The boy shrugged. "The sigils on the walls call into the earth. Or into wherever they're directed."

"What're the sigils?"

"Words and representations of words. I dunno. I can't read them."

"So both of those spires are conduits?"

The boy rubbed the side of his face, squinting at the black shapes. "Sometimes the conduit and the vessel are the same, or near to each other like those. And whatever they capture or hold comes through to the town. Or the big cities. Wherever they're directed by the words on the walls. And you power things like that sentinel in the shop. The sentinel's a vessel too. A small one though. A lesser class because it can only do one thing."

He tried to grasp the meaning of these words, though spoken in his language by this Ba'Suon boy. But like a mirage, the meaning faded the longer he looked. "Vessel?"

"The conduits are like needles that draw blood, and the vessel is like the body that holds the blood. But we don't really understand their mythicism. Mama says it's very different from hers."

"Ba'Suon don't possess mythicism."

The boy hesitated, then seemed to decide on something. He looked Janan in the eyes. "My father used to say his people simply codified what my mother's people know from birth. Mazoön enastramyths make the conduits and the vessels. They train in schools to learn it, but you and my mother... you just know."

"Hm. These 'enastramyths' made the artillery that fired upon us in the war. And the armor that protected their soldiers. But I didn't know the extent of their work." His gaze drifted back to the spires again. He remembered the shores of Té'er, the ashen rock, the sludge gray sea. He didn't look into mirrors, but he saw his own reflection in the way people looked at him. Even Prita in those first few moments in the prison. The shock of it. The confusion. For a fraction of time, she hadn't known what he'd become, what this mythicism had done to him. "She told you about Ba'Suon knowing."

"Yeah. I don't really feel things like you do though. I guess that's from my papa's blood."

"Being Ba'Suon isn't just about our knowing. I see you with your rose suon."

From the way the boy tried not to smile, it was as if he'd just praised him. Perhaps he had. It was no small thing to understand the suon.

"I know your mother was granted the land here by the Mazoön government, but how do you two survive?"

An older gentleman paused on the walkway outside of the general store. Tall, slender, in a fine burgundy suit with flowing arms, the cuffs and collar gilded with an intricate pattern of threading so clean it could be discerned even from a distance. He stared across the street at them. Omala didn't notice and talked on.

"She gives medicine to people and their animals. Does some small healings. Folks are generous with their coin as it's a rare skill this far from the cities where we don't get medical enastramyths. So what we don't gain by hunting she can buy at the store. When I was younger, she worked with our suon to find gold and silver. We got a little but nowadays all the veins have been tapped out."

The man began to cross the street with an easy gait. He didn't look to either side of him. People on horseback stopped for him. Running children avoided him. Even the suon seemed to keep their distance, arcing away from him overhead. His steps barely stirred the ground. Omala's voice trailed off when he spied the approach.

"That's Eben Wisterel," he murmured, just as the gentleman stopped within intimate speaking distance.

"Afternoon." He spoke in the Ba'Suon trade tongue, as smooth as his accent. He removed his broad felt hat and held it in his hands, smiling first at Janan, then at Omala, and back to Janan. Dark eyes with some strange reddish tint akin to his clothes. Clean-shaven and tanned. Short gold-dust colored hair, but not as clipped as a Ba'Suon woman's. A man of society despite this distant desert location. "We had heard Sephihalé Prita was bringing back her kin, but I must admit you are not who we were expecting."

"We?" Janan said.

"The town. But me personally. You are…" The direct gaze wandered all over him, "…quite the sight." They were of a similar height and something in this man's eyes told Janan that it mattered.

He didn't respond, only continued to smoke. They watched each other.

"Your dragon," Eben Wisterel said, his smile broadening. His eyes darted to the side as if Tourmaline stood there. "The golden one on the outskirts. She's also quite the sight. A magnificent creature of extraordinary power."

Janan flicked his ash and handed the cigarette to Omala.

"I would be much obliged if you would visit me on my ranch. It's east of here, beyond the spider trees. Can't miss it from the air. Do you accept my invitation?"

"Why?"

"It's not often we get a Ba'Suon so fresh from Kattaka. Not in my humble town. I'd love to hear about your experiences, to learn about your relationship with the dragons. And share with you a feast for a proper welcome to Mazemoor."

"But who are you?"

The question seemed to take him aback, this man Eben Wisterel. He touched his palm to his own chest. "You stand in the town that I built, my dear."

"So you are a builder of towns?"

"That's one way of looking at it. My business is very lucrative and I consider myself a man of vision."

Janan looked down the long stretch of street. He saw no great vision there. Wisterel waited but when he did not continue the conversation, the dragon baron smiled.

"If you're so curious, I would be pleased to answer all of your questions at my ranch."

"I thank you, but I decline."

"Now, don't be too hasty."

Prita emerged from the general store behind Eben Wisterel, bags in arms. He turned his head slightly as if he'd seen her, but he didn't lay eyes on her.

Instead he looked at Omala. "Why don't you go help your mother, son?"

The boy looked at Janan. He lifted his chin at the boy and Omala flicked the cigarette and jumped down from the fence to walk toward his mother. She'd stopped and was now staring across the street at them, beyond her son's approaching figure.

Janan looked back at Eben Wisterel. Through the prick of mythicism constantly sitting in his mind like a collar, something else thrummed. It came from this man like the sudden change of pressure from a great height. Wisterel stepped closer. His hands slowly turned the hat in his grip.

"At least tell me your name, if you won't accept my kind invitation."

"Sephihalé ele Janan."

It was like watching a starving man take his first sip of spring water. The dark eyes with their strange copper tint almost fluttered.

"Thank you. I'm sure I'll see you again."

He stepped back once and bowed his chin, then turned away, setting his hat back upon his head as he strode down the street toward nothing specific at all. Like a wanderer through an empty field. Like a man with no responsibilities or expectations from the world.

Prita approached. Janan reached for the heavy-laden bags.

"What was that about?"

"He invited me to dinner."

She looked after Eben Wisterel. "Did he?"

"I think he was really inviting Tourmaline." They began to walk toward their suon, the energetic presence of them, with the wary regard of the two smaller ones as Tourmaline played with some sort of desert rodent on the ground, her tail whipping up the dirt.

"You needn't go," Prita said.

"I declined. But maybe I'll go after all. He runs this part of Mazemoor, doesn't he? He must want something. If he wants something, we'd best find out what it is before the wanting comes up behind us when we're ill-prepared."

WHEN THEY LANDED back on the spread, a young woman was sitting on the porch. She arose as they unloaded the suon and turned them out to the land. Tourmaline wanted to fly again but Janan rested his hand along her neck and watched as the woman approached. She was small and dark, with short hair shot through with tiny round metal rings swept back off her forehead. Her arms were tucked up the billowing sleeves of her lightweight coat. A feeling of thin sharpness came to him, like a blade. She bowed at the neck to both of them but addressed Janan in his dialect.

"Drere Janan, I'm agent Phinia Dellerm'el, the caseworker assigned to you from Internal Security."

"You don't need to address me as drere."

Tourmaline swung her head around to peer down at the agent, who flicked her eyes up toward the suon and quickly looked away. She greeted Prita by name and after a moment Prita gestured to the house.

"Come." She said something to Omala in Mazoön and the boy picked up one of the supply bags and headed to the barn, looking back at them as they moved toward the house.

Janan took up the other bags. Inside, he set his rifle by the door and began to unload the items: various fruits and vegetables, grain, and sugar. The agent sat at the table as Prita set a kettle to boil water.

"So you went into town. I thought I saw your dragon but wasn't sure it was you. You were quite high in the air."

Janan glanced at her but didn't reply.

"Settling in all right?"

"Well enough."

The agent waited until he had no more items to put away. "Met Eben Wisterel?"

Prita poured the tea, watching them. Janan leaned against the sink. "Why?"

"Because a man like that can't see a man like you, and a dragon like yours, and not want to be known."

"A man like me?"

She smiled like this was some public truth. "Dangerous."

"I'm not dangerous."

Agent Phinia Dellerm'el tilted her head at him as if seeing him anew. Or pretending to. She accepted the tea from Prita and set the cup on the table without sipping. Steam rose in a twisting pattern toward the ceiling. "We both know your war record. It's why my government is having you watched."

"By you."

"Not just by me."

He looked out the window. "Those silos. The black spires. They track me somehow. Like the stud in my suon's ear."

"Indeed they do."

"Will they always?"

"No. Just until we know you can be trusted." Now she lifted the teacup and sipped. "I will always be straight with you if you're straight with me. We'll be seeing each other a lot for the next year. Do we agree?"

"And what of this man Eben Wisterel?"

"What of him?"

"You said a man like him."

"He too is dangerous."

"How?"

"He envies what you have and what you are."

"Landless and on a leash?"

She laughed. "Sometimes the land can be a leash. Ask your sister. Ask *him* when you speak to him again."

"Parceled land isn't the land I'm talking about."

He and Prita both watched this woman. She conceded his words with a small shrug that might have been agreement, might have been defense. She drank more of the tea and nodded as if consulting herself on the taste of it. "I'll be staying in the village at the inn. For a week, maybe more, on and off. Sometimes, I'll come by unannounced, like now. Other times, we can arrange a time to meet." She looked around the room as if locking images of the details into her mind. Like one of their recordkeepers, but with conscious intention. When she was finished with both her tea and her stock of the home, she stood and inclined her chin to Prita and to him. "I would like to hear you say that you will be honest with me, Sephihalé ele Janan."

He returned the nod enough to be polite. "It's not my inclination to lie. So I will be honest."

"Thank you. And thank you for the tea, Sephihalé ele Prita. I'll see myself out."

Janan watched her leave. Prita followed her to the door but not onto the porch. Through the window he saw the agent untether her horse from where she'd hitched it at the corral post, and mount up. The horse shied a little from the verbal attention of the crown. Janan couldn't see the suon but he heard them. Tourmaline had flown or else she would have probably harassed the stranger in their midst. But the Mazoön agent was free to come and go as she pleased and she nudged her horse into a gallop back to Wister.

Prita shut the door and looked at him. "Be careful what you say to them. The Mazoön of authority."

"I am."

"No. I mean be careful of your precise words. They

trade in words. They learn our languages in their universities so they can know *our* words. They build their cities upon their understanding of words in some intricate manner I have yet to understand. The marks on their spires allow their power to travel distances. To know when you come and go, and to feel your suon's disposition."

"Their spires could not make them win a war against Kattaka, not when Ba'Suon fought against them. Their enastramyths' power didn't allow them to get too far into the north, or across the long waters to the Kattakan homeland. So there are limits to their mythicism."

"Yes. But not inside their own borders. Not even Hetram could truly explain it to me. It's very far from our ways."

He turned to the sink to wash his hands, but it could not remove the grit of this new world, how it seemed to sift through the pores of his skin like sand. "We are very far from our ways here."

AFTER DINNER HE sat out on the porch again to take his smoke. It might become an evening habit as the stars here proved bright and true just as much as in the north. Tourmaline returned from her hunt and lay with her chin on her forelegs just to the left of the house, her tail carving slowly along the ground. Her thoughts were quiet, barricaded. They sat in their separate spheres of mute stillness, but he knew they were feeling the same thing. Their new world possessed a specific shape of loss.

The other suon had retreated to the aviary. They seemed to find some comfort in it. When Omala joined him on the step, chewing on a mint leaf, he asked the boy about it. "We don't keep aviaries in Ba'Suon camps. Our suon would never stay in them."

"The suon here have been domesticated for a long time. At least these kind. They don't mind it."

"Maybe they're reflecting the people around them. I've never met a suon that didn't remain wild somehow."

They sat in silence for a spell, watching the way the night seemed to change depth the longer they stared into it.

Then Omala said, "Who did you leave in Kattaka?"

Maybe it was the late hour, his full belly. The weariness of the day and how, at the end of such days, he always seemed to miss Lilley the strongest. "My harwan."

"Beloved."

He nodded once.

The boy was quiet. Then, "I miss my father."

"How did he die?"

Omala looked away toward Tourmaline. After a moment, she turned her head and regarded him with her single eye. Breath expelled between her sharp teeth in a soft chuff. Even when the boy looked down at his hands, the suon continued to stare. Listening. "He was a wrangler for the dragons at Eben Wisterel's ranch. Wisterel's got a large talon. We call them talons here, not crowns like the Ba'Suon. One of the dragons was bad business. Nobody could control it. It went sour one day and attacked." He looked up at Janan, a strange question in his eyes. Perhaps he wanted to fathom death from a soldier, not knowing that there was no reason to it beyond its inevitability. "Mama says Father was good with dragons though. Almost like a Ba'Suon. This one just turned on him for no reason, it seemed."

"Maybe it didn't want to be in the crown. They aren't herd animals, they won't all get along and rarely will they follow another suon unless it's a king or queen who has asserted its dominance. Nor will they always obey even so. Eben Wisterel should have freed it if he couldn't bond it to the crown. I'm sorry your father had to pay with his life."

The boy nodded and seemed to gather some inner resolve. Not so much a boy, now, in the way he expected answers from the other man on his land. "Maybe Wisterel wants you to work with his talon. Would you do it?"

"No."

"Why not?" The question sounded like a test. But something more resounded beneath the surface challenge. A need to understand in all ways, like the roots of an ill tree reaching for others of its kind for nourishment.

He offered what remained of his cigarette. "I will no longer be under anyone's command."

Omala took the smoke and sipped the end,

straightening his shoulders back. A little heat seemed to burn and reach out from the center of his chest, unseen to the eye. But Janan felt its fire. "I don't wanna be either."

"You are Ba'Suon, Omalasha. You possess the knowing of the cosmos, the age of generations. Like the suon themselves."

"I'm half Ba'Suon."

"Only to a Mazoön, perhaps." He looked the boy in the eyes. Seeing a grief as dark as the night, but nothing like the war he knew. Yet loss made all darkness equal in the heart. "My harwan is Kattakan. With him, there is no divide under the stars."

"Why didn't he come with you? Mama says she would've gone anywhere with my father."

The weight of that story fell heavily on his shoulders, or else he paid it too much attention in the asking of the question. The weight never did leave; he only shifted it out of his sight from time to time. "Maybe I'll want to say those words aloud at another time." He stood. "Right now I'm going to sit with my suon."

"Tourmaline scares me but I still want to ride her."

He pressed his hand to the boy's shoulder. "That's another reason I know you're more Ba'Suon than Mazoön. But you can never force the suon."

THEY DIDN'T SIT for long. When he saw all but one of the lights wink out in the windows of the house, he climbed astride Tourmaline's back and they arrowed toward the moon. All those months in the Mazoön prison he'd yearned for this—the cold air on the heights and the effortless lift of their bodies in concert as the suon's great wings arched and the hollows of the golden scales sang them through the sky. His stomach dipped and rose with their flight, the fingers of exhilaration stroking his insides like he stroked the smooth lines of Tourmaline's neck. She bellowed and it echoed from plateau to train tracks stretching from horizon to horizon. The emergence of stars in the velvet fold of night. The cosmos above in bearded streaks of white and blue. He thought of Lilley's big laugh in flights like this and how at first his Kattakan had been wary of Tourmaline, just like Omala, but over time Janan would find him nestled in the circle of a foreleg, both of them asleep between battles.

He prompted Tourmaline toward the east, overshooting the town. Below, the shadowed puddles of sparse spider trees dotted the land. Beyond them a constellation of yellow lights in regular intervals, illuminating an expansive property, an estate of large and small buildings made of pale imported stone so perfectly cast they created an illusion of carved mountains jutting from the desert, the footstool of some foreign god. Three domed roofs of russet tile. Ten tall silos stood as sentinels or as a type of border, and the closer they flew to them, the more agitated Tourmaline became. The pressure behind his eyes bloomed and elbowed to the edges of his skull like some trapped insect trying to burst from its cocoon.

A dozen horses locked in a corral some distance from the main house began to run and stamp, and Janan nudged Tourmaline higher in the sky. Below the vise of those black silos, something else ran through him like a cold shiver and he laid his chest along Tourmaline's neck and spoke to her in their own language.

She dipped low toward the biggest of the outer buildings, a barn-like structure made of the same black stone as the silos. As they sailed over its pyramid roof, the world sank into a soundless, featureless abyss. A space of nothing wherein he could not feel his own heart beating or if he even breathed at all.

IN THE MORNING he lingered over his breakfast of cornflats and spiced beans and waited for Omala to leave the table for his chores at the aviary and barn. Prita mentioned building another bed today and he nodded and talked a little about the spare lumber she kept in the barn and his ability with a hammer and nails. She seemed to remember he was not all that adept and they teased each other over the last of the coffee before he finally said, "There's something strange at Wisterel's ranch."

She stopped her cup of coffee half-way to her lips. "Why do you say that?"

"When was the last time you were out there?"

"I haven't been since Hetram died. Five years. Omala said he told you how."

He nodded. "Tourmaline and I flew over Wisterel's

estate. There's a structure on the land. Maybe it's his aviary, he's supposed to have a crown, but I didn't see or sense any suon. And this structure…"

"It's like a barn? That is where he keeps his suon at night. During the day they are on the land."

"Are his wranglers that good that these suon don't fly away?" Hetram may have been, but Mazoön as a whole did not have a true understanding of suon that he'd seen. Not in the war, at least.

"They're tame. Bred for generations to keep close to their home, which the ranch has become. He also uses mythicism, somehow, to keep the suon close."

"That 'barn' didn't feel like a barn. Or an aviary."

"What did it feel like?"

"Like nothing at all. It spooked even Tourmaline."

"What do you mean 'nothing'?"

"Like nothing, sister. Like an absence. Like there was never something there to begin with." He looked into the dark dregs of his coffee. "I've only ever felt that one other time. Like something against the nature of our world."

"When?"

"There was a man. I suppose he's still alive. A man from the north, even further north than our land. My harwan and I fought alongside him. I had thought him destitute. Longing. We took him in. I tried to know him but he always had a… a wall."

"Ba'Suon?"

"Yes. But…" He reached out his hand to take one of hers. Not for her comfort, but for his own. He listened to his heart beat for a minute as he tried to rearrange his memories into an order that didn't pierce their present peace. "The absence I felt in this man from the far north meant destruction. Foolishly I thought I could somehow alleviate it for him. Ease his suffering, his isolation. But in the end, I think he only knows destruction. It's twisted him up inside, disemboweled whatever is left of his Ba'Suon nature and turned it inside out." Sometimes, he was reluctant to even conjure Raka's image in his mind, as if the very thought of him would open some sort of channel through which the other man could reach. More than just the memory of their last confrontation. Prita looked at him with patience but he could see she didn't fully understand. "It's because of him that my harwan isn't here with me. So I think that whatever is causing that absence on Wisterel's ranch… it will only lead to destruction. Whatever he is doing there is against the nature we know."

She was silent. She searched his eyes as if the strange pale green of them could reflect her own thoughts. Or maybe she saw nothing at all. She slowly drew back and shook her head.

"Janan. Devisha. Whatever Wisterel is doing on his estate, we can't interfere. You can't."

"There is something wrong there, Prita."

"He's powerful, devisha. He knows people in the Mazoön government. He is wealthy and connected—and you are under probation."

All truths. He looked at his too-pale hands on the table and traced a whorl in the wood.

"You need to focus on other things," said Prita.

He looked up.

"Like your clothes. Yours are beginning to stink. You're a little taller than Hetram but his should fit. I'll bring them out." She smiled at him, but the edges held remembrances of sadness and new worries. Their common paths in this new world. She rose and moved behind the felt curtain around the beds. He heard her open a trunk.

At home, in a Ba'Suon camp, he would never wear a dead man's clothes. He almost told her to stop, that he would go into town and buy something Mazoön; he would wear this world and pretend he was a part of it for as long as it took for him to hunt another animal, take its meat and skin, and fashion a world closer to the one he'd left behind.

But he remained quiet. What he wore was ultimately just the shell and it wouldn't change the hollow core that rattled with every breath he drew in this land.

HE FOUND OMALA grooming one of the horses in the barn and asked if he'd like to accompany him into town. "We can ride them instead of the suon. I need to pick up some things before I build my bed."

The boy nodded. "I'll saddle them."

The sun followed them like a burning eye, as if they were trespassing on this desert. He felt the heat prick the back of his neck, the light heavy on his eyelids. He didn't talk and Omala seemed to sense it in him and kept his usual questions to himself. They tethered the horses in the center street, virtually unseen by the citizens this time. He wore one of Hetram's wide-sleeved Mazoön shirts, deep blue with white flowers on the edges. It made him blend a little more into the people, though once he and Omala stepped into the hat shop, another sentinel, like in the general store, began to squawk. He'd left his guns behind but still wore his Ba'Suon blades.

"You can't wear those in here," said the shopkeeper. Omala translated for him.

"I'm Ba'Suon."

"I don't care. No weapons."

He walked to the wall where hung an arrangement of wide-brimmed hats of all colors and sizes and decorations. The shopkeeper spoke again behind him, his words like needles. Omala didn't need to translate.

"It's quite all right," said another voice, in the Ba'Suon trade tongue.

He turned. Eben Wisterel stood in the doorway. He tipped his burgundy hat to Janan and approached. The shopkeeper didn't protest again. Omala hovered by Janan's shoulder, eyeing the dragon baron.

"Your sister doesn't often wear her blades, so I'm afraid my people don't quite understand their significance."

Janan lifted down a dove-gray hat with a slight upturned brim and tried it on. "And you do?"

"I'd like to think so. I know that you earn your blades when you tame a dragon."

He did not think Wisterel could feel his disdain the way a Ba'Suon could, or that he could exert the force of it when the Mazoön tether pressed in on his knowing, but he sounded the space between them with intent, uninterested in even meeting the man's stare. He removed the hat and touched along the buckled band. "You don't know shit."

The dragon baron seemed undeterred. "I'd like to learn."

"Why?"

"Because our people have been separated for too long, don't you think? There's much we could learn from each other. There is value in your relationship with the dragons, and I have, after all, a ranch of them. My government is wrong to fear this relationship. I believe we can open each other's eyes—a man like you and a man like me."

He set the hat back on its rack and finally turned to Eben Wisterel. "You think highly of yourself."

For some reason this made Wisterel smile. "Have you reconsidered my dinner invitation? I should mention I've also invited your caseworker, Phinia Dellerm'el. I believe we should all get to know one another since she'll be a frequent guest in Wister. Of course, your sister is invited too but I'm afraid my ranch holds too many memories for her, so I would understand if she declined." The copper gaze found Omala, who remained by Janan's shoulder. "You may come too, young man. You look old enough to work with the dragons. Maybe you can show my foreman what you've got. If you're intuitive like your father I should like to hire you on."

The boy's lip curled with rebellion. "Have you got better control of them?"

Wisterel's eyes froze on him. "You evince some pluck."

"I'll come to your dinner," Janan said.

The dragon baron's regard came slow, but he bowed, his smile lingering, his gaze angled to the floor in a display of respect. "Let's say next week from today, just before sunset?"

Janan nodded. When they were alone again, Omala said in their familial dialect, "You think he meant it when he invited me?"

He picked up another hat. Hide brown like the color of the desert. "I'm sure he did. If he can use you in some way, he will."

THAT EVENING, AFTER building Janan's bed and eating dinner, all three of them flew their suon to the red mesa south of the spread. The suon called to one another, the two smaller ones looping around Tourmaline in playful deference. She arrowed straight, more soar than fling, and blew fire at the indigo glow of the horizon simply for the fanfare. He felt the heat of it streak across his skin like the breath of angered spirits. They set down on the tableland. The endless flats were blanketed below with a quilt of shadow and moonlight, and the beach of stars above drew his thoughts to what was possible and what remained, the tide of him reaching and receding from all knowing in a constant back and forth. He breathed and turned north where, too far away, he tried to know if Lilley was asleep or awake. He couldn't feel either reality. Tourmaline rippled understanding toward him in waves of *sunset red.*

He and his family sat on the edge of the mesa and looked down the drop while the rose and red-black suon skipped along the ground. Tourmaline paced a short distance away and marked her presence. She bellowed once toward the firefly cluster that was the town, then settled on her hindquarters behind Janan's shoulder to observe the night, tenting her wings to block the gusts of breeze from troubling him at this height. He reached up to rub her jaw. Below their feet on a jut of rock he saw black and white paintings carousing in the angled shapes of people, suon, and stars. The stories of their ancient ancestors imprinted in the land for the night sky to witness.

"Will you come to Wisterel's dinner?" he asked his sister.

"No," Prita said.

"I want to go," Omala said, sitting between them. "See what he's about."

"No," she said. "The less that man notices you, the better."

"Why?"

"What do you feel when he's near?" Prita said.

Omala looked at Janan, at his mother. "Feel?"

"Your Ba'Suon knowing. Listen to it."

Behind them, the homestead suon talked to each other in short trills and rumbles. Tourmaline chuffed in momentary contentment. On the heights, the Mazoön pressure seemed less. Omala's feet swayed over the edge of the cliff.

"Think of our conversation today," Janan prompted.

"It's like he always wants something," the boy said slowly. "Like when he talks to you or looks at you, he wants more from you than whatever you say or do."

"That's a true knowing," Janan said. "You feel it pulling at the center of your chest."

"His eyes are a strange color."

"I had thought it might just be a Mazoön trait."

"Not any that I've seen," said Prita. "But then I haven't met every Mazoön."

Janan looked across at her. "Have you been to many places in this land?"

"A couple of the cities like Té'er. More of the towns here in the southern region. But not many, considering how numerous they are."

"How many Ba'Suon camps?"

"I don't know the exact number, but a handful. No more than five, I should think. We're allowed to find paths but they aren't as free as how we lived in the north. Before Kattaka. Many of the Mazoön towns or cities don't want a camp of Ba'Suon near their living. So the families have communicated which paths are amenable by mark."

"What's a mark?" said Omala.

"Carvings on the land," Janan said. "Symbols we

carve into objects on the land, like rocks or trees, to tell other families if the path is good."

"You understand," said Prita, "that the families here aren't like what we know. So many of us came here in bits and pieces, like shale. In the beginning, we were just happy to find another Ba'Suon. To hear any news that might have traveled with them, of what became of our families in the north. Who had died and who was lost. Here the families feel…"

"Broken," he said.

She nodded, her eyes limned by moonlight.

"I fear for the suon."

Her head tilted. "Why?"

"They farm them. Keep large crowns like Wisterel. This isn't natural."

"This is a different land now. They've been doing it for as long as we've been on our paths in the north. The suon here are different."

"How many are free on the land?"

"There's no way to know."

He stared down at the village of Wister.

"Is it no better here than in Kattaka?" Omala said. "Are you sorry you left?"

"Do you remember I mentioned the pit suon?"

"Yeah."

"In Kattaka, they make the suon fight each other. For sport. They eat the ones that become too ruined to fight. Sometimes they hunt them just for food. Here in Mazemoor they don't do that, instead they defang the suon so completely they almost forget their true natures. In order to make them agreeable. In order to breed them for big sales."

He stroked Tourmaline's nose until she bowed her chin completely over his shoulder and stretched her neck to peer down the side of the mesa, her breath hot against the side of his face. Omala shifted beside him, and she turned her blind eye toward him. A subtle growing curiosity about this young man who felt in some way like he and Lilley had at the start of their war more than ten years ago. The young image of them, wary but curious about each other, drifted through her mind and touched the edges of his own.

The distance inside of him widened like a wailing cave. Speaking now would send his sorrow back to his own ears. But he said, "I don't regret coming here, though it wasn't entirely by choice. Maybe it's better, Omalasha, but as your mother said—maybe it's just different."

HIS SLEEP WAS restless and haunted by Lilley. It was like lying down with a ghost. Phantom warmth and conjured touches that dissipated with consciousness until he just stared up at the deep blue light spread across the ceiling from the open window. Despite the comfort of his new bed, he rolled out, pulled on his dead man's clothes, and went outside to the porch to sit and smoke. Tourmaline was gone on a hunt and the small crown slept in the aviary, their breathing like faint bellows and the occasional flutter of their wings in dream. He removed his harwa and turned it slowly in his hands. The pearl reflected the moon in silver and white. Smoke from the burning end of his cigarette coiled up to the stars as if in praise. These were the cigarettes Lilley smoked. He was almost out of the couple of packs he had left from the prison. After that he would also lose the taste of the man.

At dawn, the agent rode her horse onto the property. It was a lean chestnut gelding with a black mane, different from the other one she'd brought. Tourmaline had returned from her hunt a short while ago, her muzzle stained with blood. The horse paid no mind to Tourmaline, who sat up from her settle near the aviary to watch them arrive. The sun melted its pink and orange light across the land. If the rose suon flew it would blend into the sky. The agent stopped her horse near Janan as he still sat on the porch steps. She looked down at him with some curious surprise.

"You're up early," said Phinia Dellerm'el.

"You come out all this way just to get a free meal in the morning?"

"Are you offering?"

"Not particularly. Prita's still asleep but they should be getting up soon."

"I came to see you."

"I reckoned."

She got down from her horse and let the reins hang. "I was willing to wait and enjoy the view."

He gestured with his cigarette toward the brightening horizon. "There it is."

She didn't look at the sky. She tucked her hands inside opposite sleeves of her shirt. Beneath the yellow hem of it he saw the shape of a holstered gun. "So we're to dine with Eben Wisterel next week."

"That's the rumor."

"Maybe he just wants to hear your war stories, but my guess is he wants to take a good look at your dragon. And you."

"I won't be riding Tourmaline to his ranch."

"You know something's wrong there, don't you?"

He looked up at her where she still stood over him. "Do I?"

"What does your Ba'Suon knowing tell you?"

He pulled on his smoke. "It tells me to keep my opinions to myself in Mazemoor since I'm on probation."

Phinia Dellerm'el moved to sit beside him on the porch. Tourmaline rose to her feet and walked over, wings unfolded and tail arched skyward like a scorpion. The agent, her mouth open to speak, snapped it shut and watched the suon approach. Dust stirred beneath the heavy steps. Tourmaline stopped near the chestnut horse and reared her shoulders back to look down at it. The horse snorted, tossed his head, and backed up a couple paces.

"Don't let her eat my horse," said the agent.

"She does as she pleases."

"Sephihalé."

He raised his chin at the suon. Blew a slow stream of smoke. Tourmaline sat on her haunches. She turned her attention from the horse to the agent, her scarred eye a fixed and unblinking regard. Janan said, "That's the best I can do. You should speak quickly and go on about your business."

"You're my business. I want to know what you've gleaned about Wisterel and his ranch. You went there, didn't you?"

"From the air."

"And?"

"It's big."

"That's your professional impression as a soldier of Kattaka?"

"Are you hiring me in a professional capacity?"

"I might. It would decrease your probation quite significantly."

He looked at her and slowly mashed the butt of his cigarette into the weathered wood of the porch step. "What do you want?"

"I want to know what your finely tuned Ba'Suon senses have gleaned about Eben Wisterel's ranch. And about Eben Wisterel. I want you to think of that when we dine there."

"Your people have so much of this." He waved his hand toward the village. "Those black silos with the markings all over them. The ability to press on my knowing and track my suon. The power to know when anything or anyone breaches your borders, even into the long waters. You think your mythicism superior to Ba'Suon ways, yet here you sit demanding my impressions of one of your people?" He stood and Tourmaline joined him, carving her tail slowly through the air until its arrowed end pointed toward the agent. "Glean it yourself."

Phinia Dellerm'el stood beside him, her hands now free of her sleeves. She didn't look at the suon but it was the kind of ignoring that meant she was fully aware of it. Tourmaline knew it too and slowly exhaled. Heat curled toward them. "Wisterel's powerful," said the agent. "But I think you know that."

"You're in the government. Speak to your people."

"I don't mean in just that way. He possesses a form of mythicism that we can't seem to penetrate."

He stared into her eyes. She didn't break. So perhaps she truly meant her truthtelling. He could feel nothing untoward but that didn't mean she wasn't also good at hiding. "So what of it?"

"So we want to know why."

"Did you think to ask him? Maybe he'll be as honest as you."

She didn't speak for a moment. Then she smiled. It held the shape of her gun.

The door slid open behind them. Prita said, "Good morning, Agent Dellerm'el. Will you be joining us for repast?"

The agent's stare lingered on Janan, then finally turned to Prita. "No ma'am. I thank you but I'll be on my way now." She looked back at Janan. "I'll see you next week."

"Apparently."

She walked to her horse and climbed up on it.

Tourmaline took a step toward them and peeled back her lips to show her fangs. A juddering rumble echoed up from deep in her throat. The agent wheeled her nervous mount away and rode at a gallop toward the village. As soon as she was out of sight the suon chuffed and turned her muzzle beneath her wing to scratch with her teeth.

"What was that about?" Prita said.

He joined his sister in the doorway where she stood. "I don't fully know yet. But none of it's good."

OVER THE DAYS he developed a sedate routine of early mornings, chores with the animals, flights with Tourmaline to explore the land, and the occasional jaunt into town. Sometimes his family joined him, sometimes he tarried with the sun alone. One night they ate in the tavern and listened to a trio of musicians and their stringed instruments ply some raucous tunes. He laughed at Omala's dancing and couldn't recall the last time he'd felt such a thrum in his throat. When the boy pulled him off his seat he only barely managed to resist. The three of them in their separate towers of shadows seemed to become lighter in togetherness, a truth everlasting beneath the stars of their Ba'Suon ancestors. The vitality of community. He imagined Lilley leaping upon the musicians' stage to accompany them with his infernal harmonica playing. For a few moments in that tavern amongst the only family he had in this country, he could imagine an alternate present, one where his harwan had accompanied him south. Though a hollow reflection of his desires, the fantasy at least resounded with a type of warmth.

The morning of the dinner at Wisterel's ranch, he joined Omala at the crown when the boy emerged from the house to rub down the suon and examine their paneling and their eyes and mouths for any signs of sickness or disease. They fluttered freely around the dry grass and bare ground, but came when called. Janan took one of the cloths from a water bucket nearby and stroked the silver suon until her scales reflected the sun like struck metal. He watched as the boy coaxed the suon one by one to extend their wings and gently brushed the translucent skin with its delicate layer of fine hairs to free it of mites. Omala possessed a sure touch and spoke quietly to the creatures. The way he stood on the balls of his feet to whisper into the suon's ears reminded Janan of Lilley's constant insistence to treat Tourmaline like she was his bosom companion. He used to admonish his harwan that one day the suon would take umbrage with such familiarity and bite off his ear. Early on, it had been a sheen of jealousy that drove his caution. Later, when Tourmaline stood guard over them in the night, he encouraged this strange friendship between Kattakan and suon. She didn't belong to either of them, after all, but chose her association. Perhaps her bonding with Lilley was to teach him this lesson.

He looked away from Omala now, but he felt the boy watching him when he stroked under the chin of the silver. She bobbed her head back and cawed with playful acknowledgment.

He asked the boy about the suon, sensing that Omala wanted to show off his knowledge in some way. Omala told him that they mainly rode the rose and the crimson-black, but the other three they flew sometimes for supply runs, or when they went hunting and camping for days on the land. In the beginning, Prita had gathered suon for Eben Wisterel, but she had not done so in years, not since Hetram. In turn, the boy asked when and how Janan had found Tourmaline.

"I gathered her when I was thirteen, from a valley our family would encamp in every summer."

"Thirteen? A suon her size?"

"It's sometimes easier for a child to gather a suon. There's no deception in the way children interact with them. But the fear has to be controlled. If they sense fear they can't trust you."

"Is it true they remember through generations?"

"It's so."

Omala leaned his shoulder to the rose suon's ribs and she nodded her head a few times as if to encourage him. Even though these smaller cousins were large enough to ride, Tourmaline would be three times their height if she stood beside them now. He saw Omala calculating this truth with what he'd just learned of gathering. "So Tourmaline's ancestors and your ancestors might've known one another. She might remember your family?"

"We do. I sensed that from her in the beginning.

That's another reason it's possible to gather them. We recognize one another. We both understand the rite. The Ba'Suon with our knowing, and the suon with their memories. It's a covenant. The way the Mazoön do it goes against nature."

"The talon, you mean."

"The breeding."

"Are you sure you want to know what's going on at Wisterel's ranch?"

He stopped his stroking hand on the silver's muzzle. The boy didn't seem so young then. "Do you know?"

"No. But now that you're here, if you do something that'll get you into trouble, what'll that do to my mother? To us?"

"I won't get her into trouble."

"What if I did go to work on his ranch? I might be able to discover—"

"No."

They watched each other. Omala's jaw wound up like he wanted to tear the flesh off a rib bone. "I love the suon too. These five are my family."

"I don't doubt it."

"If he's doing something with his talon and it got my father killed, I have a right to know."

"If he's doing something with his crown and it got your father killed, what makes you think you could assist? You can't even look my suon in the eye."

The challenge hung in the air like fog. The boy twisted the washcloth in his hand. "So I have to show Tourmaline I'm not afraid."

"If you wish to confront any suon who might go sour on you, it's so." He stepped away from the silver when the golden shard of Tourmaline's body winked against the egg-blue sky. He tilted back his new hat to peer beyond the brim as she arrowed straight to his position. She held a kill in her talons and alighted near them, tossing up a torrent of dirt. Her foretalons dropped the antelope carcass on the ground in front of him and she bellowed and flung back her wings in a proud display. Pearlescent white flashed across his vision as her wings blocked out the horizon. The smaller suon scattered, flitting back to the aviary and the roof of the house. Tourmaline tilted her head to cast her one-eyed gaze down toward him and the boy. He crouched over the antelope and passed his palm over the pale brown hide. She'd been careful not to rip it. He would be able to skin it clean and offer her the meat.

He looked up to see Omala hold out his hand to her. The boy stood very still. Her long black tongue—the length of a man's arm—rolled out and flickered over his palm. He didn't move. His other hand clutched the washcloth. She lowered her head and stared at him from the side of her face with the good eye. An exhalation of smoke curled from her nostrils. The air around them swirled with the scent of burning metal, and Janan knew that she intended to test the boy's mettle. She had done the same to Lilley, sensing something in the Kattakan long ago that conjured an inclination to know. The way suon could *know*, 'seeing' past the surface of crude shapes and steady mortal decay. Janan didn't interfere now, like he hadn't then.

She raised her chin and bared her fangs at Omala, but he had yet to move. His hand stayed out. She snapped at it, and he blinked, but his feet remained firm on the ground. Janan rested his hands on the hilts of his blades but said nothing to her in any of their mutual languages. She stepped closer to the boy and pushed her muzzle against his chest, the length of her head equal to Omala's height, but he held himself and slowly rested his palm between her eyes where the scales were flattest and smallest, and he rubbed up to her brows and between her ears. She rumbled from low in her throat.

The day changed around them. Shimmers of the air became lighter, and Janan felt the urge to bring the boy and his suon close to his chest. Tourmaline was telling him *i and gold in sun and dawn*—her gentle call for Lilley—and it spread through his body like grasping fingers. The feeling made a fist around his heart and almost pulled him to the ground. But Lilley was nowhere that he could answer her. She flung back her head and turned her flank to the boy and launched herself into the air. The wind of it nearly tossed them off their feet.

Omala was breathless when he looked at Janan. But his eyes were bright. "What was that?"

He looked back at the antelope carcass and pulled one of his blades. His back to his young brother. The pressure behind his eyes came from more than the Mazoön tether. "You remind her of someone."

PRITA WANTED HIM to go into town to buy some formal attire for the dinner. He was content with his Ba'Suon skins, so he scrubbed them inside and out with lemon water and soap, and hung them in the sun to dry. He shone and buffed the scales until they glinted like fine metals, and as the light was heading toward the western horizon, he dressed and sharpened and polished his blades and belted them to his hips. He paused at the honor table and knelt and gestured from his chest to the stars. Here he slept in the home this man had built and now he was going to the place in which he'd died. Prita squeezed his shoulder from behind and embraced him when he stood.

Omala said he could ride the rose suon but he chose instead the silver for the time he'd spent with her already, and his sister and young brother watched him catch her reins and step from her outstretched foreleg to sit astride her back. Prita didn't tell him to be careful, but it was in her eyes. He raised his chin to them and pushed into the sky.

He flew low enough to stir the dust and scrub of the land until Eben Wisterel's estate thrust into view like icebergs from the shadowed sea of the desert. With the black structure at the northern edge that swallowed the world in its whirlpool. The ten spires that pummeled their mythicism like children's fists behind his eyes.

This was why he refused to bring Tourmaline here—
to be pained by the Mazoön intrusion and scrutinized
by its proprietor.

Below, a couple dozen suon were let loose on the
land, on the opposite side of the property from the
horses. He could not see any tethers, but they didn't
fly—only pecked at the ground and skipped over one
another like river stones across water. He landed the
silver suon in front of the wide wooden doors of the
estate house. A terrace of balconies arched above him
in four levels, white stone overflowing with potted
greenery and strategically placed golden light. A sweet
floral scent drifted down to him.

Eben Wisterel and Phinia Dellerm'el emerged
from the mansion. The dragon baron hailed him as
he dismounted and dropped the reins. A woman—
perhaps some sort of servant—in patternless dark
clothes came up to bow and take the suon in hand.

"She'll be rubbed down and fed," said Wisterel.
"Please be welcome." He stepped forward to nod his
chin and open his arm as if to take Janan into it, but
instead gestured widely to indicate his ranch. "Would
you like a tour?"

"If it pleases you."

The agent stepped forward and they acknowledged
each other with a look. Wisterel led them toward the
open range suon. The horizon sank bloodless behind
them, muting their array of colors.

"It would honor me if you perused my talon and
offered your thoughts. My dragons are prized from

here to Té'er."

"Is this all of them?"

"Not in the least. This is only a tenth."

Janan paused on the clear side of the fence and looked at the crown as they flickered and trilled. Their presence ghosted along the edges of his knowing but otherwise remained muffled. No impressions of what they felt, no feeling or reaction to his scent, nor what they surely gleaned—as all suon should—was Tourmaline's imprint on his knowing. He didn't seem to exist to them.

Behind him he felt an approach and turned his chin to see a line of a dozen rough-attired people position themselves along the fence. Hats pulled low and dirt on the shoulders of their coats. Wisterel said they were his wranglers. Maybe his entire outfit, but it was impossible to tell. Janan ignored them and looked back at the crown. He stepped up on the lowest rung of the fence and stretched out his hand to the closest suon. A rust-colored male with long black whiskers fanning back from his cheeks and brows. Tapered ears. The suon paced close, slow, a curious arc of his tail. The fox-like eyes regarded Janan without blinking.

"Why are they all so blank?" he asked Eben Wisterel.

"Blank?"

He looked past the russet male to a dappled gray female who sat on her haunches and nibbled furiously at the curve beneath her foreleg. Her wings flat.

"They have no thoughts," he said.

The wranglers murmured. Some of them laughed

into their collars. They understood the trade tongue of the Ba'Suon.

"Do dragons have thoughts?" Wisterel said.

"More than you or me at any given time."

"Do you hear them?"

"It's not like that." He stared at this crown. Two dozen that were only a tenth. All of them some level of absent. Like the black structure.

"What is it like?"

He turned away from the crown and pointed to the black building. "What's in there?"

Wisterel's gaze was as unblinking as the suon. "That's the enclosure where I keep them at night."

"Can I see it?"

"Let's go in to eat. My chef has put together quite the menu, and he would be most displeased if we let it languish."

The wranglers melted into the descending night. Janan and the agent followed Eben Wisterel through the twin doors of the house and into an inner courtyard resplendent with hanging vegetation, intricate mosaics of brightly colored suon on the walls and floor, and tall doorways curved at their apex to mirror the silhouette of the house itself. Gold lined the edges of the mosaic panels. Their steps tapped clearly on the pale stone tiles. Tiny, striated rocks polished to a high sheen lined their path from courtyard to chambers, where engraved sconces trapped shadows of artistry between the glow of red lanterns. The dark wood floors so smooth it was like walking on ice, and the white walls of the interior engraved with similar sigils to those he'd seen on the pillars in the village.

The pall and pressure of mythicism that had accompanied him from the prison to this desert land ebbed away into nothing. The subtle fog of it dissipated from behind his eyes and when he blinked, the colors and scents of this mansion seemed to inhale with him and expand beyond the edges of his knowing. Become brighter. Louder. A flood of nausea rushed through him as if he had suddenly dropped from a steep incline into someone else's emotions. Amusement. Caution. Suspicion. They were coming from Wisterel and the agent, and he lacked any ability to sift them in his release from the mythicism. His walking died away to a halt and he pressed a hand to the wall. The nausea sloughed off him but he struggled to braid his unshackled knowing into sense. The agent kept going until she realized he was no longer beside her and stopped also. Eben Wisterel paused at the end of the grand hall, a wide arching doorway behind him leading into gold light and shadow. He turned to them both. He was smiling.

"What have you done?" Janan said.

Phinia Dellerm'el looked between them. "What?" she said.

"*He* knows."

The dragon baron walked back toward him. His narrow silhouette in long lines of emerald and gold that touched the toes of his velvet boots. Flared sleeves cuffed with gold embroidery and pink silk. His hands bejeweled by rings whose glaring brilliance pricked behind Janan's eyes with a different kind of pain. Wisterel set his hands on both of Janan's shoulders and didn't allow him to step back. His grip was strong. Janan pushed at the man's wrists but could not break the hold. Wisterel stared into his face with copper eyes. Any more violence, he knew, would place him in danger. More than what existed now between them.

"You told me your name," said Eben Wisterel. "To give your true name freely to an enastramyth with intent, like myself, gives them a door to dominion over it. The Ba'Suon are such a straightforward people. I wasn't confident it would work but your name possesses your essence like I hoped it would. I was able to use it to neutralize the awful tether these people put on you." His eyes flicked to the agent.

"Wisterel," Dellerm'el said. "No."

Now Janan stepped back out of the hold. Wisterel let him. "You put my name into your mythicism?"

"After a fashion. There are a series of written patterns that I had to resolve through your language and mine, beginning with your name. There are so many magnitudes of energy contained in a name. Indeed, contained in a word, in a concept. You really have no idea how mythicism operates compared to your Ba'Suon knowledge, do you? It took some work to find the right combination of logomyth patterns, even for something as simple as eliminating a tether, but you are free of them now, Sephihalé Janan."

"You can't do that," the agent said.

"Oh, it's done. I can free your suon too, Janan, if

you would only tell me her real name. I do wish you'd flown her here."

"My superiors will know," the agent said. "And they'll come for you. You have no business interfering in the work of the State."

"They'd be welcome," said Wisterel, iron now in his tone. "Let's not be hypocritical. A government-sanctioned enastramyth took his name in subterfuge when he first landed on our shores, and thus used it to tether him until now."

The agent took a single step toward the dragon baron. "That is not for you to judge."

"They'll revoke my probation," Janan said. The tendrils of this impact seemed to run through his fingers before he could grasp them. "They'll expel me from their land. My sister too."

"No," said Wisterel. "They won't."

"Unless?"

The dragon baron smiled again. "Put away your anger, both of you, and let us dine."

THE SLOW CIRCUS of food that came to them on platters of silver and porcelain possessed such fragrance and color he saw the manifestations of it all like dancing spirits in his vision. Thin slices of meat and steamed vegetables coated in butter, fresh flat bread sprinkled with spices, aromatic cream and stewed rice. Across from him at the round table, with its abalone inlay like the waters in which the cooked fish had once lived, Eben Wisterel watched him through every sip of purple wine. The agent seated at the dragon baron's right hand didn't touch her wine and only picked at the food. Janan sampled the steak before he realized it was suon meat. Then he didn't touch the food at all. Wisterel acted like he didn't notice and must not have cared either way.

"I know you don't look kindly on my practices with the dragons, but I would like you to listen."

Janan stared at the other man, one hand resting on the hilt of his blade below the table.

"My grandfather used to tell me this story," said Eben Wisterel, "which he said had been passed down through the Greatmothers of our ancestors. It is the story of Kamzaneen and the First Dragon, or what your people call the suon. Do you know it?"

"I know the Ba'Suon telling of it."

"I doubt it has much diverged, but here it is as the Mazoön claim. Kamzaneen was a young shepherd of her family in the high hills. One day, she was caught in an unexpected rainstorm that scattered her flock. Some were even lost down rock fissures and died. As winter was approaching, she knew that her family would need every single animal to survive; past winters had been growing increasingly worse and all the families in the land were struggling through the harsh seasons. In her attempt to gather her disparate flock, she came upon a dragon camouflaged in the mountain. He spoke to her and asked her why she was wandering in the hills in the rain, for he considered the towering green land as his own territory. At first, Kamzaneen was struck with awe. She had never seen such a beautiful creature. His spine looked made of diamonds and his eyes were like the molten sun. When he extended his wings, they blocked the rain for a mile. But soon she began to be afraid because of his size and the great burning of his breath that spoke of fires deep within his chest. She tried to run away but he set his great foot on the land, and the talons, which were as large as the tallest trees, barred her way. He asked her again why she was wandering in the rain in his territory. She looked into his dread eyes and confessed that she had lost her flock and should she fail to gather them, her family and other families with whom they shared survival would starve through the long winter. She addressed him as Greatfather and begged him to release her so that she may search for her flock. The dragon Greatfather took pity upon her and rather than kill her for trespassing on his territory or send her on her way to stumble in the rain, he plucked her up with one of his talons and set her on his back. He promised to help her find her sheep and so flew aloft into the sky." Eben Wisterel paused and took another sip of his wine. "Do you know how it ends?"

The dining hall had grown dim around the edges. It seemed the sconce light and the chandelier's crystal lace pattern over the table illuminated only its master. "Greatfather, who could speak to all of the creatures in the land, sounded the world for her flock and reunited them," said Janan. "When Nanee ele Kamsa returned to her family and they heard her story, the people promised to honor the kindness of Greatfather forever, and so the Ba'Suon and the suon have lived in covenant through generations beneath the stars."

"Indeed. And what do we take from such a story, Sephihalé Janan?"

"It is because of Greatfather's compassion that our people survive, and all of nature continues in this way. There is no divide between us, as the stars deem it."

"That is one interpretation."

He watched the dragon baron.

"As my grandfather told it, the story of Kamzaneen depicts the transition of our people from struggle on the land to an embracing of change. If Greatfather hadn't found the flock for Kamzaneen, she likely would have perished in the hills along with her sheep. It's an allegory of the futility of the old ways and the birth of the new. The dragon represents the power of the land, of nature, and our ability—even our birthright—to take hold of it. To ride its back."

"You twist our history."

"You misread it, and so you've been stuck in your ways and overrun by foreign powers."

"All tides recede, all storms abate, no matter how powerful."

"You think the Kattakans will simply up and leave your land? Come now, Janan. As a soldier of Kattaka you know that to be a false hope. You have witnessed the worst of nature, and it resides in people. There is no retreat from that. There is no peace from that."

His chest seemed unable to release a full breath. "Nature will always rebalance itself. But it's a fool who flies headfirst into a hurricane."

"And yet the only way to survive such massive acts of nature is often to drive headfirst into it. To turn your flank to it spells certain demise."

"I've seen the land that you claim is your birthright. It's dying. What of your power then?"

"My people, too, are stuck in their ways." The dragon baron looked at the agent for the first time since they were seated. "Don't you agree, Phinia?"

"Then what does your future look like, Eben?" said the agent.

"Ah. So now we come to it." Eben Wisterel stood. He laid his white napkin on the table beside his half-eaten feast plate. Wine from his lips stained the linen. "Follow me and I'll show you."

AT FIRST, JANAN didn't know what he was looking at inside the black building, the false barn that swallowed all senses into a pit from which there could be no recovery. With his own knowing now untethered he felt the suction of all awareness leaving his body the moment Eben Wisterel shut the heavy doors behind them, and somehow this building tore away what was so recently recovered. He saw on the left side of the vaulted room cages of suon huddled together in shadow, and on the right side more suon impaled to the walls like specimens of curiosity. They writhed and squealed, a sound he had never heard from any suon. On the walls, everywhere, the ceiling, the floor, those markings of mythicism carved into the black, and the gold glow of it disgorged from the engravings like lava surging from the bowels of the earth.

The suffering, trapped inside this mausoleum and pulled apart by the markings, seemed to bulge and burst and bulge in a continuous, throbbing beat. Suffering congealed within the confines of this prison, the scent of it all black rot. His body began to shake.

"We possess an unending supply of power that need not drain the land," Eben Wisterel was saying. "We can breed this supply. But the smaller species require constant quick renewal. A larger dragon would provide more for less effort. The Ba'Suon are the only people who can capture the northern dragons, is that not so?"

"Janan, no!"

He didn't hear the agent. He pulled his blades and trapped Wisterel in his arms, tight against his chest. He pressed the sharp edge of one blade to the dragon baron's throat and the other in a vertical line from heart to gut.

"Open the door," he said to the agent.

"Janan—"

"Open the fucking door!"

Phinia Dellerm'el pushed the doors wide and he maneuvered Wisterel to the outside, keeping the agent in his line of sight and his back to the exterior wall. Wisterel's hands remained out as if to ward off some attacking animal or else to warn the night of madness.

The wranglers stood in a loose ring facing them. All were armed. The agent removed her sidearm from the folds of her long coat.

"What do you think is happening here?" said Wisterel.

He breathed. The desperate sorrow and stain clawed at his back from within the black building. The thick viscous gasp of slow death. "You're going to remove my name from your mythicism or I will gut you open right here in the dirt."

"Think, Sephihalé. Even your caseworker knows this won't get you anywhere but in my service. You drew a weapon on a citizen of Mazemoor. I can dictate your fate. And your sister's."

"Your fate should be the one you're concerned with."

From over the dark desert, his battle suon bellowed.

Nobody moved. He waited as Tourmaline winged closer, the cadence of her flight the low pummel of war drums, her beating wings, the wind through her scales a scream that punctured the night. Her gold scales flickered in the silver moonlight like flashes of lightning from the depths of thunderclouds. The wranglers looked up, their guns out. Rifles. Shotguns. Some would carry dragonshot, but none could penetrate Tourmaline's armor. It would take a cannon.

Wisterel remained a taut form in the lock of Janan's arms. "What do you propose to do with that dragon?"

"You will free those suon or she will burn this land to fucking cinders."

"It's not that simple. Either of your requests. I can't just scratch your name from the walls or my notes and reverse the change. You can even burn my house to the ground and it wouldn't reverse it. What has entered the world can only be converted, not removed entirely. It will take some time." The man seemed to relax against him, bend into him like a lover, not a prisoner. "In the meantime, you'll be mine. And if you want your sister and her son to be immune to the consequences of your actions, you'll convince your dragon to succumb. There is no releasing my talon. Some of these little ones are owed to people more powerful than me."

"Let him go," said the agent. She stepped close to Wisterel and pressed the mouth of her gun against his temple. "Janan, let him go." To the wranglers: "All of you, put your weapons down and step back." She pushed the gun until the dragon baron's head tilted to the side. "Now."

"Are you also making futile decisions, Phinia?" said Wisterel.

"Janan, let the bastard go. He's right about your name."

Janan looked at the agent and didn't move. Tourmaline alighted on the barn's roof and shot fire over their heads, her talons digging into the black stone, crumbling pieces to the ground. The wranglers ducked even though the flames carried well above them. But the heat of it bathed them all in a stifling wash. Her bellow split the air and cowered all but the three locked in a tableau. The wranglers set down their weapons and moved back from the suon as she arched toward them with her long neck, her ears and wings back. Her tail risen.

He slowly released Eben Wisterel, who stepped from his grasp and stretched his shoulders to an unbending height. When he turned to Janan he was smiling, all but his eyes.

"Get your dragons," the agent said to Janan. "And go back to your sister. I'll meet you."

"There's no other way this will end," said Wisterel.

Tourmaline could free the suon within. She felt the suffering too and blazed her rage toward the Mazoön. But Phinia Dellerm'el was staring at him, and her eyes said, *Not now.*

He raised his blades to his suon and she launched from the roof of the mausoleum—for that was what it was—and landed like an earthquake on the ground beside him, scattering the wranglers and forcing the dragon baron and the agent to stumble back. Dust rose and danced. He holstered the blades and his suon lowered her foreleg and he stepped up and onto her back. Her tail whipped and felled Wisterel to the packed earth as he ducked to avoid it. Janan sounded the estate for the silver suon and as Tourmaline launched herself toward the stars, the smaller cousin joined them from the crown left out on the range. Her lighter trills pricked the night beneath Tourmaline's deafening battle cry.

*   *   *

PRITA AND OMALA met him by the horse corral when he landed Tourmaline and the silver. The horses were in the barn. The crown in their aviary greeted the silver suon, but they settled uneasily under the force of his turmoil. The night sank quiet and he didn't need to speak. Even the boy likely felt the distress rolling off him like a thick fog. Tourmaline arrowed back into the sky as soon as he was clear and began to circle the homestead as guardian, occasionally bellowing a warning to the east where Eben Wisterel's ranch pulsed out of sight, though not without its presence reaching even miles toward him like an echo.

"He is using those suon," Janan said before his sister could ask. "As some sort of power source. They are mounted on the walls of that black building like trophies and he is somehow…"

Prita didn't approach him. His upset meshed with rage, and she held herself and her son well back.

"Where is the agent?" she said.

"She told me to go. Said she'd come back here."

"What did you do?"

He didn't answer.

"Janan, I need to know if we should expect a Mazoön posse."

"No. I don't think so. Dellerm'el possesses some sort of authority that even Wisterel won't cross. But I put my blades to him."

Omala crouched on the ground and set his hands into his hair.

"Did you cut him?" Prita wasn't asking as a form of reprimand. Her eyes burned with a deep fire.

"No."

"Come inside," his sister said. "Both of you."

She made tea but nobody drank. Omala sat on top of the table and Janan leaned against the sink, his hands curled back against its edge.

"He bound my name in his mythicism."

Prita looked at him, wordless.

Omala lifted his head. "What does that mean?"

He kept looking at his sister. "He removed whatever means the government was using to keep track of me. He did it to prove that he has the power to change aspects of my being because he possesses my name."

Prita turned to face the honor table. He watched her back expand as she breathed and regarded the tokens of love and remembrance for her harwan.

"Can it be undone?" said Omala.

"I don't know," he said.

"You are battle trained," his sister said, still facing the candles. They mimicked the flames of stars. "So is your suon. A northern suon of the Ba'Suon, whose ways are not the ways of Mazemoor mythicism. And you, a man who's fought Mazoön forces and survived. Even bested them. The agent was right."

He knew it.

"You and your suon both sensed something on his ranch that none of us could. That's the power he wants."

"He can't get it," said Omala.

Nobody replied to him.

"That bastard can't get it, Janan."

"He has me already," he said. "And if not him, then Mazemoor itself. And I've pulled you both into it."

Prita said, "The suon?"

"I couldn't do anything. I had him against my blades, but he won. He knew what he was doing to show me the suffering of his crown. To provoke me. And I fell right into it."

Her eyes glittered diamond-hard in the dim light. "Then we might as well go all the way and free those suon."

He just looked at her. Omala sat up straight.

She went on as if he'd protested. "Your actions reflect on me regardless. I will gladly leave this land if it means first stopping the suon from being exploited. Or from allowing my devisha to be commanded by a man such as this."

"He has at least a dozen wranglers in his outfit. And over two hundred suon. Even with Tourmaline, we can't take him on right now. I won't kill his crown if he sets them against us. The agent said she will come. I want to hear what she has to say." All bad decisions in battle arose from rash action.

Omala got down from the table and disappeared behind the drapery that separated them from the beds. He heard a kick of frustration against the wall.

"I won't leave them to suffer," he said. "No matter what."

"Neither will I," his sister said.

*　　*　　*

PHINIA DELLERM'EL ARRIVED at dawn, riding her chestnut gelding. Janan was sitting on the porch smoking. Every time he thought of the suon on that wall he trembled. Tourmaline still circled overhead on watch. The agent looked up at the golden suon, then she looked at Janan and got down from her horse. She dropped the reins to let them hang and walked up the porch and right past him to the door. "Let's talk."

Prita was sharpening her blades at the table with her stone. She nodded to the stove where the kettle piped. He picked three cups from the countertop and asked after Omala. His sister said Omala was in the barn taking care of the chickens, so he made three cups of chrysanthemum tea and brought them to the table. The agent was sitting there already and watched Prita with the blades. They were obsidian and emerald, and the suon bone shone to a reflection. Prita didn't touch the tea, and he just held the cup in his palms to warm himself.

"Now you understand why we need you," said the agent.

"I understand why Wisterel wants me. But I don't want either of you."

"You don't have that option now. At the very least we can't allow him to keep you in the boundaries of his mythicism, nor can we afford to have your dragon in his grasp. He's developed his skills in a way that runs counter to what the government finds acceptable. We can't let this continue."

"So you object to his using the suon in this way?"

"Yes, we do. It's illegal."

"But you dig into the earth and draw from the waters. You didn't see someone like him deciding to use living creatures in this way?"

She frowned at him. "We have laws. He broke them. The problem is he has allies in the government. In business. He has people with a vested interest in developing our mythicism in this manner."

"You condone exploitation and create competition, that's why."

She waved her hand. "This isn't the time for Ba'Suon philosophy. You should be more interested in how you won't end up like those dragons, nailed to the wall for his use."

"I'd kill him before that ever happened. I don't care what the fuck your laws say."

"I'm going to pretend I didn't hear that."

"You do that."

"Right this second, he can be working on a way to make it impossible for you to harm him. In fact, I can guarantee it. Fortunately, it can take weeks to write a pattern against someone's will that would be in any way effective, even knowing your true name. But we still have to move quickly."

"We?"

"I've sent word to my superior. They want me to offer you an alternative and if you accept, it will go through."

Prita blew on the edge of her blade and raised it to the light. He looked at its perfect edge. He looked back at the agent.

"What is it?"

"From the moment you crossed our borders we've had our eyes on you. You fought under Lord Shearoji."

"I won't fight for you. My war is over."

"We don't need that kind of fight from you. We want you to help us root out people like Eben Wisterel. It would only be for the duration of your probation, then we would revisit your status here in our country. Same as we did for your sister."

He looked at Prita. She set her blade on the table. Listening. Letting this Mazoön woman talk.

"Why haven't you asked people like my sister, who have been here all this time?"

"Not every Ba'Suon has your sensitivity to mythicism. Nor your battle dragon. We saw that in the prison. We put pressure on it to gauge your reactions." She paused and watched him for a long moment. "How did you know something was wrong with his talon? That building?"

"Because," he said, "it negates nature as we know it."

"How's that?"

"I told Prita… I've felt it before. From a man I knew in the north. A Ba'Suon from the far north. He's the reason I'm here and I realized such possession can't be penetrated. Instead it swallows all knowing as we understand it. Somehow Eben Wisterel has created that same absence through your mythicism."

"What did he do? This man from the far north?"

Sitting at this table, in his sister's home in the desert, he felt very distant. The present moment drained away and even the surface of the table seemed foreign to his eyes. His hands on the wood not his own hands. The harwa on his wrist an indictment rather than a symbol of bonding.

He shared a tattoo with Lilley, inked by a kusha of his people who they'd met on a joint mission with another Kattakan unit. Two years into their war and he knew he never wanted to be separated from Lilley, that somehow this Kattakan stood with him looking at a common horizon and it would always be so. They'd both been young when their war started. Ten years they fought together. They bled for each other. They bed down together. Lilley's family going back generations were slaves to the ruling class they now fought to defend and the irony of both their situations grew a sharp humor between them. And love.

The ring of stars, the cosmos of joining, circled on his shoulder. And on Lilley its twin. *Belonging to all, beloved of one.* An oath made permanent. When the war receded to treaty, he offered his harwa. Not only would Lilley be bonded to him, but wearing the harwa would connect him forever to the generations of Sephihalé right back to the time of Greatfather. He was the only blood child of his parents. Lilley touched the sea pearl. From the seriousness of his expression Janan knew he understood the giving. They lay in the canvas tent that had been their home through years of war. The exterior cold pushed against the small heat from the lamp they burned but they were warm beneath layers of fur and the shared space of each other's bodies.

"I can't accept this now," Lilley said, a somber shadow in the pale blue of his eyes.

"Why not?"

"It ain't that I don't feel it. You know I do. But I want you to give it to me when we're free of this place. Free of the army and all this bloodshed. Free of my people. I want you to give it to me in witness of your family and the stars. Full ceremony. The way it's supposed to be done."

He wondered now, in the desert of Mazemoor, if his harwan regretted that decision. At the time he understood that Lilley wanted to honor his family, to honor the Ba'Suon. When would his family ever be reunited now? He looked at the Mazoön agent. The demand in her eyes. The expectation of things for which she had no right to ask. Not so different from Eben Wisterel.

He spoke as much to Prita as he did to Phinia Dellerm'el. Since by the end of the day they both might find themselves in different circumstances. He owed this to his sister.

"His name's Abhvihin ele Raka. He fought alongside my harwan and I, against your people. Raka began to consider my harwan his own, and he and I had conflict about it sometimes. Because I knew he could be dangerous." This was no longer a recurring dream, the memory of it refused to be obscured. As he spoke the words, the reality came back to him like an inevitable winter from the turning of a season. Cold and shadows enveloped him. "When my harwan and I planned to leave Kattaka, he refused to go with us even though I offered. I thought if only he was away from Kattaka, he could be healed. He and I argued about this plan. In order to stop us he stole this from me." He laid his arm on the table. His wrist. The harwa ringed around it. "This is an artifact that's been passed down through generations of my family. I mean to give it to my harwan. Raka was jealous, so he took it and gave it to Lord Sheoroji as a prize. My harwan and I wouldn't leave Kattaka without it and this is what Raka anticipated. When we attempted to take it back, Raka exposed our plan to Shearoji. In the fight that ensued, only Tourmaline and I managed to escape. And I came here."

His sister reached across the table and took his hand. Her grip was warm but couldn't warm him. He continued to stare at the Mazoön agent.

"You want what doesn't belong to you. Same as Wisterel. Same as Raka. This want swallows all else. You don't see… none of you see that it's all the same thing. Your destructive need to take even from the very nature that preserves you. With Raka and with that… place… on Wisterel's ranch, it's a physical thing. Maybe Wisterel's mythicism that created it can be broken, but I'd found no way to negotiate Raka's void. So unless you want me to kill Wisterel outright so that I may free his suon, whatever else you ask of me is a sacrifice I'm unwilling to give again. It will end in loss and I'm here already, far from my people, our land. Far from my harwan. I've lost enough."

The agent leaned back, her hands dropping below the table. "I sympathize with what your people have endured. But should Wisterel and enastramyths like him be allowed to develop this harmful style of mythicism, it won't work out for anyone. Least of all the Ba'Suon, who you see he covets greatly. So I'm afraid I can't accept your answer." She stood. "You'll agree to our proposal or those of us who *are* on your side won't have the power to keep you and your dragon out of his hands."

"I'll leave."

She looked down at him. "You can try. Both of you." Her eyes found Prita. "But I wouldn't recommend it. It's a long flight to the shore and the islands beyond, and our weapons have developed some since the end of the war. Not to mention Wisterel still has your name. If we don't force him to free you, he will propel you back here sooner or later."

They sat at the table long after the agent left. Prita didn't release his hand. She took his rage and let it dissipate through the end of her blade, which she stabbed into the wood of the table.

He looked at her. He looked around, unsure how much time had passed. "Where's Omala?"

Outside, the cloudy desert morning seemed to drop around their shoulders. A sunless cold. Tourmaline no longer flew watch overhead and when he sounded the landscape for her, she gave back an image of Wisterel's ranch. *i and wrath and little one i*

The boy was nowhere and the rose suon could not be found.

*   *   *

TOURMALINE RETURNED TO him and brought with her chaotic images of leaping fire devouring the air. To the east, black smoke spiraled to the sky. He and Prita flew to Wisterel's ranch armed with both blades and guns.

The mausoleum was an inferno. Suon clogged the air and ground, flitting directionless like bats in a storm. Some of the wranglers were attempting to haze the ones on the ground further out on the range. Horses screamed and kicked in the tumult. But these desert suon, blank to thoughts, couldn't find a leader to follow in the sudden mass of the freed crown and grew more confused by the shouts of the wranglers.

Janan pointed Tourmaline through the fracas of the crown. Let them hear and feel the strength of a queen of their kind. His suon roared, cutting through the snapping growls of the tall flames. He laid himself flat along her back and soaked up the cool sweat sifting through her hollow scales to ward away the heat of the fires. She called and the smaller suon answered. A dozen of them wheeled in her wake and darted beneath her soaring wings. A dozen more arched to nip at her tail, and yet more launched into the air away from the wranglers to catch up to their crown. They followed Tourmaline as she led them away from the crumbling mausoleum, turning west toward Prita's spread. A growing single movement against the gray sky like a murmuration of starlings.

She dipped to skim the desert floor. He leapt off her

back and ran until in propelling momentum he could turn and make his way back to Wisterel's ranch. The suon were free but his sister, on her feet, bulled her way straight through the wranglers on horseback, both her blades in hand. Her crimson-black suon was one of the few left in the sky, circling and cawing and spitting warning fire to keep the wranglers at bay. Behind it trailed Omala's rose suon.

"Where's my son?"

Janan pressed his back to hers and watched the wranglers as they wheeled and stamped their horses close by. Smoke blurred his vision and fed choking fingers down his throat.

"He's here," said Eben Wisterel. The dragon baron stepped from the house's open doors, dragging Omala by the arm, a gun pressed beneath the boy's chin.

"I freed them," said the boy. His body bent as it tried to get away from its imprisonment, even as his head and neck could not follow.

Janan aimed his rifle at the enastramyth.

"He came here with your dragon and did *this*," said Wisterel.

"Let him go."

"We're beyond that now." Wisterel shoved Omala forward and fired one shot.

Prita lunged. Her blades swept down in a concave arc. She stood in the way of Janan's aim. The boy crumpled face down on the ground bleeding from the back of his head. The wranglers began to shout. Eben Wisterel stood motionless with two bloody stumps just below the elbows where his arms used to be. His gun on the ground still lodged in his right hand's grip. Janan fired twice at the wranglers to keep them in disarray and ran forward to grab his sister's arm. He sounded wide for her suon, a sharp command of *here* and *defend* with such impact the suon landed immediately beside them and flung back his wings to throw any attacking horses off their balance.

"Go." He shoved his sister to the suon, slung his rifle and leaned down to pick up the boy.

Overhead, he heard Tourmaline bellow. She'd come back for him. The wranglers scattered, shooting wildly as her fire rained down in a protective ring around him and his sister. He draped Omala over the back of the crimson-black. Prita climbed on behind. Her eyes were white spheres, void of emotion. He shoved the smaller suon's shoulder and the crimson-black launched into the air. Tourmaline swept low. He grabbed hold of the spine of her left wing and ran himself up her foreleg and aboard her back. Her tail slashed behind them to further ban the wranglers from attack. She seized two of them in her jaws and snapped down. He and his suon cut into the sky, and she flung the mangled pulp of the bodies to the ground amongst their kind.

Below, Eben Wisterel collapsed to his knees in a widening stain of his own blood.

THEY FLEW WEST to the mesa beyond Prita's homestead and alighted far from its drop on the open tableland.

Prita dragged Omala from the back of the crimson-black and held him in her arms on the ground. The suon paced, agitated, and blew gusts of smoke. The air smelled of burning and blood. Janan knelt beside his family and pressed his hand to the boy's chest. It didn't rise, there was no heartbeat.

Prita wept. Her cries rang the world like a tolling bell.

THE SHAPES OF the freed crown speckled the stone gray sky like ash. Whether they would survive in the wild he didn't know. They flung in all directions, unsure now where to go, where to rest.

HIS EARLIEST MEMORY was of Kattakan boots trampling through his family's mata. This was before the war, when the invaders and their conqueror lord claimed only a trading interest with the Ba'Suon. His family should have known then—any guest who did not remove their boots in deference to the mata and the stars above could not be trusted.

He remembered looking down at the boots on Raka's feet as the other man stood in the tent Janan shared with Lilley. They were Kattakan boots because Raka, despite being Ba'Suon of the far north, dressed like a Kattakan. In the beginning he'd thought it simply a disguise to ease his relation to their superiors in the army. In this, their final argument, he knew that it had been a choice born of a different kind of alliance. One that only looked out for Raka's interests, Raka's desires.

"I won't go south with you," Raka said. Sometimes when he spoke, with the tight absence of himself locked around him like iron bars, it rendered his words like echo. Hollowed out of living energy, only hearing its own sound.

Janan knew this argument would end much like the others. "Why not?"

"You and Lilley have this notion—a fanciful dream—that going south will free you of everything you've experienced here. It won't."

"Oh? Do you live amongst the stars that you can discern our futures now? Maybe we only want to be free of ruling Kattakans. That much is possible."

"You have no idea how far they've reached. You don't know anything, only some rumors that Mazemoor is better. You'll trade one set of compelling for another."

"I think you don't want us to leave because you're afraid. What are you afraid of?"

Raka's dark eyes could look on the world, force complicity, and pull everything into that same darkness. Sometimes, under the force of it, Janan regretted welcoming this man to their fire. No association seemed to warm him, except for Lilley. The needling and Kattakan disregard because Lilley could not feel this void in Raka. He called the Ba'Suon man 'surly.'

Raka said, "Lilley won't go with you. Kattaka is all he's known."

"He knows me and Tourmaline. That's all he needs."

Something flickered behind the blind depths. "That's what you truly believe, isn't it? So why invite me along?"

"That's not what I meant."

How the words echoed now, if only in the confines of his own mind, here upon the tableland. That Raka had refused to believe him because, in the end, Raka was right. That despite all the war they'd shared, the three of them as a unit, he would never trust the man alone with his harwan. He would never trust that the void in Raka would not extend and swallow Lilley eventually, pull every last bit of light from his harwan into an endless abyss until nothing remained but a faint impression of the man he was, a ghost in the world.

In his insistence to tell Raka he was wrong, their argument escalated to threats. And thus the promise to defy each other congealed into something physical, a path laid that could not be revoked. What had been formed into being by words alone eventually manifested into a night of fire and loss.

And he stood in this foreign land and felt the repeat of it. The history of it spinning out like a web in permutations and patterns he could not anticipate, yet they caught him, his sister, and his dead little brother. These patterns trapped them all in paralysis.

His words, his unmaking of the world.

* * *

OMALA'S ROSE SUON tented her dawn pink wings over the body and trilled at it, rapid and urgent at first before descending to something more like whimpers. Prita walked to the closest edge of the mesa. Janan stood with Tourmaline and watched her. Eventually her legs collapsed and she sat with one hand braced to the rock, and he went over and sat beside her and wrapped his arms around her, holding her tight. In the distance, a skinny line of smoke still traced the sky. Further south, the town of Wister in detached quiet. The sun floated on its own path, obscured by clouds, and a wind whipped through them until Tourmaline crouched nearby and angled her wings.

His sister spoke. "When they imprison me for this, you must keep an honor table for him. And for Hetram."

"They won't imprison you. I will bargain. They want me, they must free you."

"They won't agree to that."

He gripped her harder. "We can run."

"You heard the agent."

"I've fought their systems of war before."

"Wisterel has your name."

"Then I'll go back and finish it. He can't do anything to me if he's dead."

"Is that how their mythicism works?" She looked at him. Her eyes still too white around the edges. The color bleached from her skin. "We aren't meant to live like this, Janan. Alone and with blood on our hands."

"It's too late to think about that."

"It's all I can think about." She looked across the land below them. The paths of their ancestors now foreign and unknowing. "The family Suonkang are in this country. They live in the Antler Mountains northwest. I should have gone to them when I was pregnant with Omala. A child should feel family around them at all times."

"You loved him. So did Hetram."

"It's not enough."

He sat with her, quiet.

He said, "I'll finish Wisterel. Then we'll find the family Suonkang, at least for a while."

"I don't want to run anymore, Janan."

When he looked toward the east, he saw the dust kicked up by a trio of horses riding at a gallop toward the mesa.

PHINIA DELLERM'EL AND two others sat on their horses in the desert below and waited for them. She sent no hail and made no gesture. Maybe some form of Mazoön mythicism had led them here but it didn't matter in the end. Janan told Prita to remain on the tableland and flew Tourmaline down to meet the riders. The horses snorted and paced as Tourmaline reared back on her haunches and fanned her wings in a display of dominance, but the riders held the reins and none of them bolted. He jumped from his suon and walked to the posse, rifle braced against his thigh. The agent dismounted and met him.

"Where is she?"

He looked toward the top of the mesa. Looked back at the agent. "Is he dead?"

"No."

"If he was dead, would it free me?"

Something in the agent's eyes flickered. A sharp recognition. "It would. Only the enastramyth with your name can wield it. But another pattern would have to be written to convert the one he used. Probably another tether that can later be released for good by the one who converted the original. That would be easiest."

"What happens if he's just dead and another pattern isn't written?"

"His work mutates unpredictably. You don't want that."

"So either way I'm tied to you people."

"We wouldn't use any pattern against you without your knowledge. Nor have we."

"But you waited until now to tell me that killing him could free me."

She didn't answer. The horses shifted behind her. The men of her posse watched him from beneath the shadows of their hat brims.

He looked toward the open land. "I'll come with you. I'll do whatever you want. But you must free Prita and give me a moment alone with him."

"I can't guarantee that, Janan. Any of it. Someone's got to answer for attacking a citizen of Mazemoor."

This is what people like this agent said when they felt they had the advantage. "I won't keep looking over my shoulder wondering if he'll figure out a way to control me."

"We won't allow him."

"You understand I can't trust you. Any of you and your fucking mythicism."

She drew a breath and set her hands on her hips and looked to the side, toward the ground. As if reading the manner of the loose sand that formed patterns over the hard-packed earth. "I thought you Ba'Suon disliked fighting."

"Don't mistake my unwillingness to fight as an inability to kill."

She turned back to him and measured him with a steady gaze. "If I give you Wisterel, your sister will still have to answer to it. Worse if he dies."

"She understands that. But he murdered her son. If there is any justice in your laws, they would consider that paid."

"Perhaps. But you aren't really in a position to bargain."

"So you're saying if I don't do what you want, you'll let him control me. But if you don't give him to me and fix what he did, we'll leave. And I'll burn every Mazoön town from here to the southern coast." He looked at the men behind her, whose horses scraped the ground. He looked back at her with a dead regard. "You can take your chances that your weapons are effective against me and my battle suon. We will go to war, and I will become everything that your government fears of me. I have nothing to lose; do you?"

She ran her tongue over her lips. Her eyes narrowed

as if she tasted something bitter. But then she turned to the men on horseback behind her and motioned sharply with her chin. She looked at him again. "Tell your sister to come down and we'll get this done."

HE LOOKED EBEN Wisterel in the eyes. Then at the bandaged stumps of his arms as he lay in a canopied bed in the upper floor of his great estate house. The opulence of silk and fine linen and woven tapestries and gold and porcelain weighed on him with the irrelevance of all material possessions at the end of life. Janan saw the realization in his countenance, a shadowed expression in the dim room. Dust floated through thin lines of sunlight angling through drawn white drapery.

"By your presence here, I can only assume you've struck a deal with the Bureau." A doctor or somebody had given the dragon baron medication for the pain. It slurred his words.

"I have."

"And you believe that they'll unknot the pattern I made of your name? Even after I'm dead?"

He didn't answer.

"My boy, you never should've come to this country."

"You shouldn't have shot my brother. Or used the suon."

Eben Wisterel turned his face to the tall windows as if to seek beyond the drapery. To will some future out of the stars only he could perceive. "Would you be a dear and let me see the sky?"

Janan stared at the man. Slowly he sat on the edge of the bed and caged his arm over the weakened body. He leaned down and caught the copper gaze as it shifted back and forth away from his face before finally locking with his eyes. He held it. With his right hand he drew the blade of suon bone from his belt.

"There will be no more sky for you," he said.

HE RODE THE train into Té'er once a week and visited Prita in the prison. Tourmaline stayed behind on the spread and routinely squabbled with the smaller suon, but they listened to her. He tended the horses and the chickens and the goats. He knelt before two honor tables and kept the candles lit. The agent and her government fit him with a sentinel, and once in a while it spat messages to him and he flew out to meet her wherever she was in the country. They ran missions on this person or that who possessed something of Wisterel's abilities and chose an illegal path. Sometimes, in these missions, she told him to kill their mark. She wrote notes and sent them back to her superiors in the Bureau of Internal Security. She had never been just a caseworker. She didn't tell him the full truth but she didn't need to. He knew. The Mazoön government, like the army, had different units and sometimes they worked at cross purposes, each believing in the righteousness of their own mandates.

He no longer wore a dead man's clothes. He skinned and scraped and tanned his own Ba'Suon tunics and trousers and sewed the scales in and relined the felt in his boots. The hat was the only Mazoön item he wore. The people on the train stared and maintained empty seats around him and the blades he set on the table with him. Dellerm'el had given him a patch to hang from his belt, an embroidered white and gold chrysanthemum on a swatch of deep purple leather that said he worked for the State Department. Nobody questioned him about his weapons.

Look at us gettin through in the world, he imagined Lilley would say. If Lilley knew what he'd become. Perhaps that was a fantastical assumption. Another dream. More likely Lilley would look at him with sorrow. *Look at what they've made you do.*

The court had allowed two days for mourning so Prita could burn her son's body and they could honor the smoke that rose to the stars. After, she was escorted by their law to the prison and he stayed on her land. In that first week he dreamed every night of Lilley and saw an apparition of Omala standing around the rose suon as if to rub her down after a flight. It was only his daylight imagination since the boy's spirit had rejoined the cosmos, but maybe it was his own guilt that conjured the revenant. Sometimes Tourmaline looked in the direction of his imaginings, spilling *i and brother redsun in cloud.* She felt it too. He'd left his harwan in a land of war, and his presence in this one had led to the death of his little brother. Death rode his shoulders like a willful child and he could not be rid of it.

He waited in the visitor's portico for the guard to escort him into the prison proper. It was Sooly, who had looked at him with controlled surprise the first time he showed for Prita. Now it was routine, and he passed on through all the doors and endured the buzzing pressure of the prison's caul on his knowing as he sat in the private room and waited for another guard to bring Prita in. They weren't allowed to touch, but she wore no shackles and only Sooly stood just inside the door to watch them, even if he looked like he wasn't paying attention.

She asked after the suon. He relayed mild stories of their antics and of the stragglers from Wisterel's ranch that still populated the desert around the stead. The ones who had been impaled on the walls by the enastramyth in his mausoleum had been killed in the fire. A mercy, though they would carry their anguish forward to future generations.

"He had a brother," Janan told her. "Who's claimed the estate, apparently, but he hasn't visited."

"Will this brother be trouble?"

"I don't know yet." He could not say in the presence of the guard that the agent had told him to watch. Prita knew anyway. "What about here?"

Though Wisterel was dead, Phinia Dellerm'el said, his allies weren't. Should someone decide to punish the Ba'Suon woman who had on record killed their enastramyth, such action could penetrate even these walls.

"It's the same," said Prita. Her face looked drawn, her

gaze grayed out as if only wintering weather embodied her spirit now. "But if you've been busy chasing their enemies, maybe that will change."

"The most insidious enemies are from within."

"This isn't our fight."

"We're here now. It might as well be."

"This is what you tell yourself?"

He couldn't lie to her. "Yes."

She asked him for a cigarette, and he took the pack and a box of matches from his hip pocket and slid out a stick. Sooly watched. He struck the match and lit the cigarette for her and passed it over. It was a Mazoön brand and tended to leave a rusted taste in his mouth, like old blood. She drew on it and leaned back with one arm across her stomach. The smoke traced the lines at the corners of her mouth and her dark amber eyes.

"These people, like the Kattakans, aren't happy unless they're at war," she said.

"I know it."

"There must be other lands somewhere."

"Probably. But they might be like this too." He watched her smoke. "When you get out, you should go to the family Suonkang in the mountains."

"Why?"

"Because you shouldn't be alone. No matter what, five years from now, go to the Suonkang."

She didn't say anything for heartbeats, only watched him. Then, "What about you?"

"I don't know where I'll be in five years. I might be dead."

"I mean now. Why don't you go there now? Sell my land. Take their money and find our people."

"You know why I can't." It wasn't all the Mazoön government.

"He tells me not to be alone."

"I have Tourmaline."

"What about your harwan? Get your agent to find a way to send a message to Kattaka."

"I've asked already. The Kattakans won't let him go. They say he's in debt to them." His hand dropped to the table. The ash-black wood. His pale unnatural skin. The harwa still on his wrist. He wanted to hold her hand. He needed the touch and breathed around the taste of cinder in his mouth, in his nose. She stared at him, like she was looking at both a form of death and an idea of life. She couldn't touch but she leaned toward him.

"Janan."

That was all she said. His name.

IN FIVE YEARS he went all up and down the country, even after his service to the government. By the second year he was off his probation, however they classified it after the warring with Eben Wisterel, and both he and Tourmaline were given leave to go where they willed just as long as they didn't stir up trouble. Mostly he and his suon encamped on the land. He built a small mata that he erected when the weather was strong. Tourmaline no longer wore the tracking stud in her ear and they released him of their monitoring, rewrote Wisterel's pattern, or so they said. He didn't feel the pressure of any surveillance, but he wasn't convinced that meant they weren't watching. Still, it was about as much freedom as he'd ever had since he was a boy.

Alone with Tourmaline in the wild, it moved through his mind more than once to fly north and find Lilley. Tourmaline herself pushed the impression through his waking hours, and more than once in his dreams. She remembered why they had fled in the first place but still she thought to fly back again. To risk the Kattakan cannons and their catapult fire. To risk the displeasure of the Mazoön government who'd taken them in. He thought of it every day, even knowing that he had no idea where Lilley would be now, as it was unlikely he would still be in Fort Nemiha. The days passed with the heaviness of this thought as he tracked the land from forest to hill.

One day in late winter they encamped by a cold rushing river the color of gunmetal. The trees hung heavy-laden with snow. Tourmaline burned a circle to steam the ground and provide a place for him to build his mata, a round just enough for two people and their gear. After, he gathered deadfall and shook a few lower branches and chopped them to make a fire. It leapt clear and high, and he sat before it and watched the flames, his coat wrapped tight around his body and his blanket around his coat with his arms tucked in against his chest. Tourmaline settled near and watched the river. They waited for the sun to set but it seemed to take some time as the clouds overhead obscured the stars, the moon, and the prospect of a swift night. A slight breeze shook the door of his mata behind him and he breathed the scent of woodsmoke and winter. He imagined it was Lilley emerging from their shelter to wrap his arms around him. *Why're you out here in the cold?*

He felt Tourmaline's attention peak before he saw her raise her head and sit back on her haunches. Her wings fanned briefly. She stared across the river and he looked. An old man had emerged from the tree line on the opposite shore. He led two horses, one for riding and the other carrying packs. He wore a long, weathered coat of matted black fur and his wide-brimmed hat was dusted with snow. His beard was the same color as the snow. He paused, holding the leads of his horses, and spied them across the river. For a minute they just watched each other, the horses stamping at the presence of the suon but steady under the old man's hand. Then the old man led the horses to the river's edge and let them drop their heads to drink.

The old man shouted across the sound of the rushing water. "That there's a big dragon."

Janan didn't reply.

"She gon eat me?"

He stood and walked to the embankment where Tourmaline had melted the snow and some mud and bracken now swirled in the moving eddies. "No," he answered, just loud enough to be heard.

"Good," said the old man. "I ain't much to eat anyway. You make sure she knows that."

The horses drank. Tourmaline flicked her tail.

"I can tell she's a female," continued the old man, crouching on his side of the river until the long ends of his coat pooled around him like a squatting animal. "From the shape of her brows."

He understood then that this man had fought in the war. He had fought suon the size of Tourmaline.

"Why're you out here, son?"

He considered his answer and what would be the simplest. And the most true. "I have nowhere else." *I have no one else.*

The old man straightened from his crouch. He turned his back and walked over to his pack horse. Janan watched him. The other horse had a rifle in a sheath strapped to the saddle. The old man ignored it and removed something from the pack horse and came back to the edge of the river. He unfolded a book of creased paper until it spanned as wide as his open arms. "You know what this is?" he called.

Janan shook his head.

"It's a map of the world, son. Not of Mazemoor. Not of Kattaka east or west. The world." The old man refolded the map until it looked once more like a book and placed it flat upon a nearby rock. "When I leave, you can fly your dragon over here and take it."

"Why?"

The old man laughed, the sound of it like shaking branches. He walked back to his horses and gathered their leads to bring their heads up from the water. "Look at me, Ba'Suon. There ain't no more time for me to see what there is to see. But I reckon a man with nowhere else to go can find some new views." He slowly wrapped the rein of the packhorse around the saddle pommel of the other horse, then he climbed aboard that horse, flicking his coat to the side. He rested his hand on a holstered pistol at his hip. But it was just a common gesture of familiarity. "Is it true that dragons think and feel like people? She ain't just a beast that you ride like these horses?"

Janan took a step closer to the water's edge. Lilley had asked him this same question when first they'd met, barely out of their boyhood and armed for war.

"Even horses think and feel," he said. "Even trees and this river and the clouds above. But they aren't the language or the emotions we know. They're of pure nature. What is your name?"

The old man laughed again. "We don't give our names in this country, my boy. I hope you find your path." And he turned his horse's head and receded back into the forest's edge.

The river rushed past, carrying voices down from the hills. A light snow began to fall as the sky pulled a curtain over the earth. Gray became indigo until the fire in front of his mata was the only light in the darkness. Even the moon hung obscured and mute. He touched Tourmaline's cheek as she arched her head over him and chuffed at the space across the river where the old man had been.

"I know," Janan said. She had recognized the old man. All suon remembered the slightest passing of time and those who moved within it. A former enemy now wandering the wild like him, tethered to nothing, perhaps to no one. Though even glancing at such a thought provoked Tourmaline to straighten and chide him. *i and redsun gold and i*

And Lilley, the whisper against his ear. *Go get that map, Janan. We're gonna need it someday.*

COME SUMMER, HE found himself in the desert again, back on Prita's old spread. He had never sold the land but he sold the animals and freed the suon, all but the crimson-black and the rose—Omala's suon—who'd waited for Prita's release from prison in a Mazoön aviary. Sometimes the others came back. The iron door of the old aviary was always kept open and swung listless in the breeze. He caught the acrid scent of fresh droppings when he landed with Tourmaline but no other sign of the long ago crown or the remnants of Wisterel's talon. Tourmaline walked a circumference around the land and pissed her mark. He went inside the house where the honor table had fallen to decay and he lit the candles once again from the few he carried with him and blew the dust from the surfaces of suon scales and wood. He arranged his belongings and his supplies by the door and took his weapons to the space behind the curtain and leaned them against the wall. That night, he lay in the bed he'd built and listened to the wind cavort through the open windows, chasing out the scent of disuse. The shadow of his suon from the swathes of moonlight pouring onto the land played across the ceiling as Tourmaline moved around outside in her own nocturnal musings.

In the morning, he went into Wister on foot and ate at the inn. The people watched him, conversation hushed. He ignored them all, and after he went down the street with its broken stones and checked at the post office. There was a letter stamped from a month ago from a town in the north of Mazemoor called Tallo. Prita often posted him from there since joining the family Suonkang in the mountains.

She'd written again.

My devisha. Lilley is here. Antler Mountains. Prita.

HE PACKED HIS belongings on Tourmaline and they flew. She barely wanted to rest, the image of **bloodred** flowed from her knowing to his like they shared one artery and his harwan was the life that propelled their flight. In three days he found the Suonkang camp in a lush green valley seated at the skirts of towering gray mountains. The silhouette of them against the remote blue sky suggested the broad palmate antlers of an alpine elk. The camp, dotted with the round shapes of a dozen mata of various sizes, lay a couple miles distant. Tourmaline bellowed and a king suon answered back.

Neither he nor Tourmaline sensed the king until his shadow fell across them. He looked up and saw the white underbelly and felt the resonant thud of its call pierce through his body. The sound of the wind fluting through the king's scales drowned out the world, then seemed to swallow it in his wake. Dragging all knowing behind him into some narrow point so dense it could have impaled time itself. Tourmaline wheeled in distress and dove to the ground to get away. The king followed, now as silent as the thin canopy of the world's upper elevations. Janan couldn't breathe in the grip of it.

Suddenly the king suon flung away from them, disappearing into the clouds. Tourmaline landed in the center of the Suonkang camp, all thunder and bellow, and whipped her tail in battle arcs. He clung to her back, fists locked around the reins. Ears ringing from his suon's cries. People had begun to gather around them, though they maintained a safe distance from Tourmaline's wings and tail.

She swung her long neck toward her hindquarters. *bloodred* He looked past the angle of her wing and saw Lilley.

His harwan wore Ba'Suon fur and quilted blue cotton with deep scarlet scales stitched into the coat. The minutiae of detail bombarded Janan's sight all at once. Lilley's red hair had grown long, but his Kattakan beard remained short, shot through with gold in patches. He looked slight of build, smaller than Janan seemed to remember, but he moved quickly forward when Janan jumped down from Tourmaline and crossed the grass toward him.

The world around them in all its fury roared and tumbled like an avalanche and he just held on.

THE SUONKANG LEFT them alone, relinquishing even common motions of greeting and courtesy. He barely noticed their going. Tourmaline walked around him and Lilley, chuffing, poking her muzzle between them so Lilley could rub and kiss it. Janan stared at him. It felt like he would never shut his eyes again for want of looking. Their bond hadn't changed—he knew it wouldn't. But he felt something else in it and could not give it a name. Maybe it was just the collision of so much emotion. The fatigue he saw in Lilley's eyes, that he felt himself. The joy. The blind relief not knowing where to rest now, when anxiety had been its prison. His hand found the long line of Lilley's back and traced it from shoulders to hip. Testing the material reality in front of him. He feared his touch would dissolve this man into ash. Lilley looked at him, pushing Tourmaline's face away. The same blue eyes he remembered, reflecting either cloud or sky. All weather, all the world.

"C'mere," Lilley said.

The kiss scattered all thoughts of illusion.

THEY SAT BY the lake that lay like a mirror for the face of the mountains. The silken water barely moved. Tourmaline made herself a tor at their backs and they leaned against her curled foreleg. He held Lilley's right hand in both of his, their shoulders pressed together. He traced the new scars he found on the knuckles. The leatherbound stump of Lilley's left arm rested on the suon's leg. They felt her breathing, content. Warm breath pushing against the cooler air rising off the lake.

"The king dragon that greeted you," Lilley said.

"Is that what he was doing? He's a part of the Suonkang's crown?"

"He's mine."

Janan looked at him. "You gathered him?"

"No. Méka did. You'll meet her. But he chose me. Raka…"

He didn't want to talk about Raka. Not so early in their reunion. But he listened.

"Raka's dead. And now he's a part of that dragon."

He'd met madness in this country. But he couldn't understand the words his harwan spoke now. That Raka could even be dead. Some part of him had always assumed the man would exist in his void-like state until some other devastation of nature would force him into life. Something no amount of companionship had ever been able to provoke, except in sparks with Lilley. He thought, somehow, that if Raka died, he would feel it like a quake deep in the earth. That it would shake the ground from sea to mountaintop. But, no, he hadn't felt anything. And now, only shock.

"Part of the suon? The diamondback?"

"Raka did this thing and now he's a part of that dragon and he's a part of me."

"What do you mean?"

Lilley shifted to face him straight on. Red light glinted off the suon scales on his coat and seemed to flicker in his eyes. "Raka killed himself and in that killing he became a part of that diamondback king and he also became a part of me. I can feel it. You can too."

A dark serpentine sense coiled between them that he'd thought was a form of grief at all the time they'd lost. Lilley continued to look at him. He stared back. Truth came to him on shadowed wings and settled on his shoulders.

"Why didn't you tell me what he was?" Lilley said.

Janan squeezed his hand. Hard. "He asked me not to. And I thought I could help him. But I was wrong, and then it was too late."

"Well he wanted me and now he's got me."

"*I* have you."

Lilley didn't answer. He looked back at the water.

Janan gripped the back of Lilley's neck, tangling his fingers in the bed of red hair. If he could shake the remnants of Raka out of Lilley, he would. What glimmers of sorrow winked for the loss of Raka's life now began to snuff out in his anger—that even in death, the Ba'Suon man could not stop taking. "*I* have you, harwan. We've had each other for fifteen years, and whatever he did doesn't change that."

"The bastard's done a lot in a short space a' time, Janan."

"We were here before him and we're here after."

"I get dreams now. Of the ice north where he's from. I can feel every mood of that king dragon. I can feel some part of him in my limbs and I wanna fuckin knock my head against a rock."

"You're already crazy, Lill. That might improve it."

Lilley blinked. Then he laughed, that big sound Janan remembered, and shoved him all the way to the ground. Tourmaline chuffed and shot her head up and looked around. For a moment, at least, they were the only ones in that place, by a lake at the feet of the mountains in a country to which neither of them laid claim. Under a sky inking ever darker until the stars appeared above and witnessed them.

As THE CAMP fell into silence, he sat outside his small mata with the door open behind him so he could hear Lilley sleeping. He smoked one of Lilley's cigarettes and looked up at the night. Tourmaline flew in lazy circles over the camp, on watch. Protective of their reunion and keeping bright in her memory the past years of fire and war. He didn't try to coax her down. Vigilance was in her nature, and probably in his too. Besides, the diamondback king also roamed the high altitude and his wariness at Janan's presence beat like a heart in the spaces between the smallest aspects of the atmosphere. Raka's suspicion, perhaps. Maybe even jealousy. Lilley told him to ignore it, so he tried. In the warmth of the mata it was easier.

Now, the cool air skated across the bare skin of his

shoulders and soothed rather than chilled. There'd
been festivities at his arrival. He'd met the Suonkang
for the first time, and reunited with Prita in a solid
unrelenting embrace. He mingled with the other
Ba'Suon who had come to Mazemoor and searched
for one another regardless of familial ties. He'd met
Suonkang ele Mékahalé, who'd freed Lilley from
slavery. A quiet woman with sharp eyes. The bond
between her and Lilley had come to him in steady
regular waves, an emphasis of the absence he and
Lilley had endured. But it was comforting to be among
his people, the fullness of a family of dozens. The air
felt swollen with the warmth, something he had not
felt in quite some time. The Ba'Suon here spoke many
dialects plus the common trade tongue of their people,
though he'd said little to anyone besides his sister and
his harwan. Some things were not for first nights.

Overhead, the plum-dark sky was dusted with the
breath of the cosmos, and he watched as meteorites
bisected the full and burning backdrop of the stars,
stitching them together. He held the cigarette between
his fingers and let it ash and just breathed the mountain
air. One constellation told the story of their beginnings,
another their possible future—the vast outreaching of
hopefulness entwined with the contiguous heart of
his knowing that all Ba'Suon shared. That he shared
with Lilley, who wore the harwa that he'd kept safe
for years. He could feel it on Lilley's wrist even sitting
distant from it. Later there would be ceremony. For
now, a coming together.

He heard Lilley rise from the bed and the drag of woolen blanket across the floor of the mata. Then both the blanket and arms wrapped around him, the warmth of Lilley's chest against his back, skin to skin. The scratch of bearded chin on the edge of his shoulder. The lake's dark face capturing the spirit of the mountains and giving it back with such clarity and peace that he thought he felt the giants in the granite sigh in recognition, in acceptance of the oncoming dawn.

ACKNOWLEDGMENTS

IT'S NO SMALL feat to tell a single story in long form over multiple books, and I owe some of the clarity of that vision to the following wonderful, talented people: my agent Tamara Kawar at DeFiore & Company, my editor Amy Borsuk at Solaris, artist Sam Gretton (because book covers are an indelible aspect of how readers begin to engage with your story), and copyeditor Charlotte Bond. Thank you to everyone at Solaris for helping to champion The Crowns of Ishia; it truly takes a village for creative work to be seen and heard.

Thank you to my family and friends; it's so much more gratifying to be able to share a dream. Thanks to my fellow writers who respect and support one another's work; all of our voices deserve to be heard. Thank you to everyone in various forms of media who signal boost and support the works of writers and artists in general; your dedication matters, especially in a world that seems to be increasingly intent on devaluing the work of creative artists.

I also want to acknowledge the tireless work of those who are vigilant to preserve our natural world and the creatures within it, whether on land or at sea. People can debate all they want about what's important in the artificial systems we've created and continue to sustain at the expense of human and other lives, but none of those systems matter if there isn't a healthy planet and ecosystems on which we can thrive. That is an intrinsic, inviolable truth. These stories are a conversation I'm having with myself, as much as they are anything else.

ABOUT THE AUTHOR

KARIN WAS BORN in South America, grew up in Canada, and worked in the Arctic. She has been a creative writing instructor, adult education teacher, and volunteer in a maximum security prison. Her novels have been translated into French, Hebrew, and Japanese, and her short stories have been published in numerous anthologies, best-of collections, and magazines. When she isn't writing, she serves at the whim of a black cat.

FIND US ONLINE!

www.rebellionpublishing.com

/solarisbooks   /solarisbks   /solarisbooks

SIGN UP TO OUR NEWSLETTER!

rebellionpublishing.com/newsletter

YOUR REVIEWS MATTER!

Enjoy this book? Got something to say?

Leave a review on Amazon, GoodReads or with your
favourite bookseller and let the world know!